"I'm sure [obscured by barcode]

She passed [obscured] him and stared out the window, her hands resting on the counter since there was nothing more to wash. "That's if I get through this mess without ending up in prison."

He set the pan aside and put his hand on hers, gave it a squeeze. "The Colby Agency is not going to allow that to happen."

She turned her hand up and entwined her fingers with his, her gaze searching his face before settling on his eyes. "Thank you. I can't imagine going through this without you. And the agency," she hastened to add.

He managed a smile when what he really wanted to do was lean down and kiss her. He sensed that she badly needed to be kissed. "I am really grateful I was the one chosen to help."

Reader Note

The first Colby Agency book, *Safe by His Side*, was released in September 2000. This book, *Witness to Murder*, marks twenty-five years of the Colbys! I hope you enjoy this story.

As always, I sometimes tweak elements of a real-life setting or situation, so don't be surprised if you notice something that is different from what you know or expect. Fiction is fun that way! Happy reading!

WITNESS TO MURDER

DEBRA WEBB

Harlequin
INTRIGUE

If you purchased this book without a cover you should be aware that this book is stolen property. It was reported as "unsold and destroyed" to the publisher, and neither the author nor the publisher has received any payment for this "stripped book."

Harlequin® INTRIGUE™

ISBN-13: 978-1-335-69025-8

Witness to Murder

Copyright © 2025 by Debra Webb

All rights reserved. No part of this book may be used or reproduced in any manner whatsoever without written permission.

Without limiting the author's and publisher's exclusive rights, any unauthorized use of this publication to train generative artificial intelligence (AI) technologies is expressly prohibited.

This is a work of fiction. Names, characters, places and incidents are either the product of the author's imagination or are used fictitiously. Any resemblance to actual persons, living or dead, businesses, companies, events or locales is entirely coincidental.

For questions and comments about the quality of this book, please contact us at CustomerService@Harlequin.com.

TM and ® are trademarks of Harlequin Enterprises ULC.

Harlequin Enterprises ULC
22 Adelaide St. West, 41st Floor
Toronto, Ontario M5H 4E3, Canada
www.Harlequin.com

Printed in Lithuania

Debra Webb is the award-winning, *USA TODAY* bestselling author of more than one hundred novels, including those in reader-favorite series Faces of Evil, the Colby Agency and Shades of Death. With more than four million books sold in numerous languages and countries, Debra has a love of storytelling that goes back to her childhood on a farm in Alabama. Visit Debra at debrawebb.com.

Books by Debra Webb

Harlequin Intrigue

Colby Agency: The Next Generation

A Colby Christmas Rescue
Alibi for Murder
Memory of Murder
Witness to Murder

Lookout Mountain Mysteries

Disappearance in Dread Hollow
Murder at Sunset Rock
A Place to Hide
Whispering Winds Widows
Peril in Piney Woods

A Winchester, Tennessee Thriller

In Self Defense
The Dark Woods
The Stranger Next Door
The Safest Lies
Witness Protection Widow
Before He Vanished
The Bone Room

Visit the Author Profile page at Harlequin.com.

CAST OF CHARACTERS

Leah Gerard—It was late at night. Did Leah really witness a murder or did she imagine it?

Owen Walker—One of the Colby Agency's finest. He is immediately drawn to Leah, but can he protect her and clear her name when every piece of evidence points to her as being a killer?

Isla Morris—Leah's best friend and roommate. She has been missing since Leah witnessed the murder. Was she murdered too?

Raymond Douglas—The victim. Was his only mistake in wanting a date with Leah Gerard? Or does he have secret troubles of his own?

Louise Douglas—The ex-wife of the victim. She has more to gain than anyone...but she has an airtight alibi.

Detective Anthony Lambert—He's a good detective...but he has secrets of his own.

Victoria Colby-Camp and Jamie Colby—Victoria could not be happier that her granddaughter has joined her at the agency. This will ensure the Colby legacy goes on for another generation.

Chapter One

*Chicago
Saturday, August 9
Chicago Chop House
La Salle Drive, 11:30 p.m.*

Leah Gerard had waited, seated at an elegantly set table in a barely lit, well-appointed dining room, for more than thirty minutes.

Many things could be done in half an hour. She could have a leisurely lunch in that same amount of time. Or she might read a couple of chapters in her current favorite book. For that matter, she could vacuum her entire apartment or have her biannual dental cleaning.

But she was doing none of those. Leah had waited thirty-three minutes, now, for her date to finish up his business meeting. And it was nearly midnight. This was not the way a first date should go.

She rolled her eyes. Honestly, if her best friend hadn't been on her back for weeks now about Leah jump-starting her social life, she would not have bothered with this date thing. Who had time for a social life when her final semester of graduate school started in just over a week? She needed every minute that she wasn't working to get a head start on the required reading. This was, admittedly, something she should have started weeks ago, but she'd taken every extra shift at work possible to build up her savings.

Between her share of rent and food, she barely scraped by. Once the semester began, she would be forced to drop back to part-time at the library. Until then, every paid hour counted. As much as she wanted to maintain her grade point average, she also wanted to eat and have a roof over her head.

She braced her elbows on the table, rested her chin in her hands and sighed. What the heck was she even doing here?

"Good question," she muttered with mounting disgust—mostly at herself.

The dining room part of the restaurant was barely lit because the place was no longer open. The Chop House had closed at ten. Cleanup had been done, and the staff had departed. Raymond, her date, had promised he would be ready to go at eleven. He'd asked Leah to meet him here so they could go straight to a nearby after-dark art exhibit that was supposedly all the rage. The gallery was only a few blocks away from the restaurant and the opening began at midnight, so they would have time for a drink before things got started.

Leah checked the time on her phone and shook her head. That would not be happening at this point. Oh well. Raymond Douglas was supposed to be a real catch. She'd met him only once and he had seemed very nice. He was certainly handsome. And he was a rising star in the culinary world. In fact, he owned 10 percent of this exclusive downtown restaurant, as well as a few others. He'd met with the other investors right here tonight and stayed after closing to work out a number of issues with management. Except, apparently, things had not gone well, or surely he would have been finished by now.

With another quick check of her cell phone, she confirmed that he had not sent a text to explain why he was running behind or how much longer he would be. She'd done exactly as he'd said she should—she'd arrived at eleven. The last of the staff had been leaving, and no one had questioned her coming in as they hurriedly departed. She assumed Raymond had informed them that he was expecting a guest. Either that, or the crew had been too tired or so happy to be off work—maybe both—that they just hadn't noticed her at all.

Leah checked the time once more: 11:40. This was inching toward ridiculous. As patient as she wanted to be, the last of that patience was swiftly running out. Five more minutes, she decided. She could give him that much time. Isla Morris, her roommate and best friend, had reminded her that Raymond was no one to blow off. Leah had googled him. She had a feeling he was more playboy than she was interested in. Frankly, she was stunned he'd called her. The one night they had run into each other was when Isla and two of their friends had taken Leah to their favorite dance club for her birthday just two weeks ago. Isla had told Leah that she had worked at the Chop House through her undergraduate premed years, which was how she'd gotten to know the guy. After the chance encounter on Leah's birthday, Raymond had called Isla and asked for Leah's contact information. And here she was.

So far the night wasn't exactly social media post worthy. Not that she posted that often. She was too busy, and frankly, she just wasn't that into online social stuff.

Next year, she told herself, life would be different. She would be finished with school, would find a great job and life would start to shape itself into a good, financially secure future.

Leah occupied herself with surveying the dimly lit dining room. Most of the lights were out, but the room wasn't completely dark. There was just enough light to give anyone who walked by on the sidewalk a glimpse of high-class dining. The tables were all dressed in fresh white linens. Crystal and silver flanked elegant white plates. All was set for lunch tomorrow. Stylish, modern chandeliers hung from the towering ceiling like icicles. Sleek black marble floors were the perfect backdrop to all the white and silver. The floor-to-ceiling windows framed the vast room like a stage for passersby to admire. It was all very chic.

Enough waiting. Leah scooted her chair back and stood. With a big breath, she walked across the room, weaving through the sea of tables. A thump startled her to a stop. Was that a door? Was he leaving the office finally? Should she go back to the table?

Another thump…then a series of dings like hanging stainless steel pots swaying together.

Leah moved closer to the swinging door that led into the kitchen area. The echo of footsteps had her expecting Raymond to walk through the door before she reached it.

But he didn't.

What was he doing in there?

She stepped closer to the door, stood on tiptoes to see through the octagon-shaped window that allowed for viewing comings and goings. Her gaze first settled on the rows of pots and pans hanging from overhead hooks.

A long stainless steel table that gleamed from its recent cleaning sat beneath them. Then...

She froze.

Blond hair...black suit jacket... Leah blinked. Raymond lay supine on the floor. The stainless steel table blocked her view of the lower half of his body. But his upper half was right there in full view. Blue shirt...darker blue tie. Her gaze settled on his face. His eyes were open. Blood made a path down his forehead.

The air stopped flowing into her lungs.

Leah blinked again to give her brain a moment to make sense of or refute what her eyes saw. Her lips parted, and a scream swelled in her throat.

Then he moved.

The scream deflated.

His upper body slid fully behind the table, out of her view, as if someone had grabbed him by the legs and pulled him away.

A smear of blood on the gray flooring was left in his wake.

Leah cupped her hand over her mouth to hold back the new scream that burgeoned.

Footsteps and another thump echoed.

Abject fear sent adrenaline rushing through her veins. *Run*.

Leah turned around to run and stalled once more.

Don't make a sound.

She forced herself to move more slowly and silently as she wove her way through the tables and toward the entrance. Her heart pounded harder with each step. Her body weak with relief, she pushed against the doors. They didn't move.

The heavy wooden set of French doors were locked.

Ice formed inside her. *What now? What now?*

She eased away from the door and the hostess station. Head spinning, she hunkered down behind a table. There had to be an emergency exit somewhere...

Think!

In the corridor where the bathrooms were located, maybe.

Or was it?

She'd never been here before, but she had gone to the ladies' room when she first arrived to check her hair and makeup. She closed her eyes and called to mind that short corridor. There had been an emergency exit there...right? *Yes.*

But that corridor was on the other side of the dining room. As she stared across the expanse now, it seemed miles away.

Another indistinct sound came from the kitchen.

Didn't matter how far to the exit...she had to get out of here.

Heart thumping wildly, she got on all fours, tugged up the skirt of the black cocktail dress she'd chosen for this date and then crawled along the floor. She couldn't risk standing up again. If whoever was back there glanced through that kitchen-door window, he would see her. She remained on all fours, rushing around and between the tables as quickly as the building terror would allow. When she reached the corridor, she almost cried out with relief.

Once she was in the short hallway, she dared to stand.

Even before she reached the emergency exit she saw the

sign. Opening the door would trigger an alarm, which the killer would hear. He would know someone was here...a potential witness.

Defeat sucked the wind out of her.

Desperate, she eased into the ladies' room. She wished there was a lock on the main door, but there was not. She hurried into one of the stalls and locked the door, for all the good that would do if someone wanted to get in. It was meager protection, but it was the best she could do. Leah drew in a steadying breath and used her cell phone to call 9-1-1.

As soon as the dispatcher was done reciting her spiel, Leah whispered, "My name is Leah Gerard. I'm at the Chop House on La Salle Drive. Someone murdered Raymond Douglas. Whoever killed him is still in the restaurant. Please...help me." A keening sound rose from the depths of her soul.

"Are you safe?" the dispatcher asked calmly.

Leah forced her mind to focus. "I... I don't know. I'm in the ladies' room, locked in a stall. I don't think he knows I'm here." She listened intently for sound beyond the room. Nothing. "Please hurry."

"Did you see or hear a weapon?"

"No," Leah murmured.

"Are you armed, Ms. Gerard?"

"No. Please. Hurry."

The dispatcher assured Leah a unit was already en route to her location. She was to stay in place and on the line until help arrived.

Then Leah did the only thing she could... She waited.

Sunday, August 10, 2:00 a.m.

FOUR UNIFORMED POLICE officers had arrived. One had stayed with Leah, taking her statement, and three had searched the entire restaurant. They had combed through the alley behind it...the dumpsters. They had scrutinized all vehicles parked in the area. Neighboring businesses had been checked, but all were closed for the night, with no signs of breaking and entering or other foul play. There was no one else on or around the property except Leah and the police.

Presumably, whoever had...*hurt* Raymond had also taken him away, completely disappearing by the time the police arrived.

Harold Manafort, the restaurant manager, had been called.

The good news was, they had not found a body.

There was no blood anywhere.

There were no signs of foul play whatsoever.

Nothing.

The bad news was that Leah looked like a fool.

She sat at a table now, only a few yards from the corridor where she'd hidden in that ladies' room for what had felt like an hour but was likely only fifteen or twenty minutes. Detective Anthony Lambert sat at the table with her, a pen poised above his notepad. He scribbled and turned pages and scribbled some more as she told her story for the second time.

She'd told it first to the female police officer who had come into the ladies' room looking for Leah after the four had forcibly entered the building. Her three fellow officers had spread out and begun the search that proved futile.

Eventually, a detective, the one now seated at the table with Leah, had arrived, and she'd repeated her story. He'd asked a few questions, and then he'd spoken with the uniformed officers and gone through the restaurant and the alley with them. A moment ago he had returned to her table and started to ask more questions. Throughout it all, the female officer, whose name Leah still could not remember, held vigil nearby. Leah wasn't sure whether they feared she would take off—obviously she could get out, now that the front entrance had been breached—or that she would call someone on her cell. She was surprised they hadn't asked for it yet. After all, she was no doubt considered suspicious at this point, seeing as how no body or blood had been found in the place where she'd insisted on having seen both.

"So," Lambert said, drawing her attention back to him, "you sat out here alone in the near darkness for forty-five minutes, waiting for your date." He leaned forward and peered at his notebook. "One Raymond Douglas."

It sounded particularly sad when he said it aloud that way. Who waited that long in a dark restaurant for a man she didn't even know—had only met briefly that one time? "Yes. He'd asked me to wait in the dining room for him and I did."

Desperate. Besides suspicious, the detective likely now believed her to be desperate.

Lambert studied her over the bifocals he'd settled into place on the bridge of his wide nose. He was not a large man. Average height, slim build. Yet it was obvious he spent some time in the gym. His arm muscles bunched and flexed against the sleeves of his shirt. He'd long ago removed the suit jacket and hung it on the back of the chair next to him.

He had keen, probing eyes. He seemed alert, ready to dive across the table and kick some butt if necessary. Not at all the cliché detective so often depicted on television. If not for his gray hair, she would never have believed the man was fifty-eight. She wouldn't have known his age had he not said something to one of the uniformed officers about being too old at fifty-eight for these sorts of calls. At this point, Leah was feeling far older than her twenty-eight years as well.

"He'd never asked you out before," Lambert said. Not really a reasonable question, because she'd explained the extent of her knowledge of Raymond Douglas already. But she'd watched enough crime dramas on television to recognize the drill. He was fishing around to see if her story would change.

"We didn't know each other before two weeks ago."

He flipped back a page and appeared to verify that his notes were correct, or maybe he was simply buying time. He looked up. "Do you understand the ramifications of making a false statement to the police?"

Leah's jaw dropped. "What?" Was he seriously asking that question? She really had not expected him to go in that direction. What kind of person did he think she was?

"We found no body. No blood. No *nothing* to suggest what you say you saw happen actually happened."

Anger flared in her belly. "I know what I saw."

"Perhaps you fell asleep while you were waiting and dreamed it." He shrugged. "It's happened to me. I fell asleep once and dreamed my wife left me. Only difference is, three days later she did."

"I did not fall asleep," Leah said, unable to keep the bitter edge out of her voice. This was bordering on ridiculous.

"Mr. Manafort said Raymond Douglas told him and the investors who came to last night's meeting that he was leaving immediately after that meeting for a long-awaited vacation."

The statement took Leah aback. "Why would he ask me to wait here for him if he was going on vacation right after his meeting?" It made no sense. This had to be a mistake.

"That's a very good question," Lambert agreed. "My first inclination is to not believe he asked you to wait."

"You think I'm lying?" A glimmer of outrage flashed through her. "Why in the world would I do that?" This was insane!

She was a full-time student who worked every minute she wasn't glued to a book or a laptop. There was no time in her schedule for games like this. There was, frankly, no time for anything. The idea of how many hours she had just wasted made her all the more furious.

So much for putting herself out there, as her roommate had insisted.

Lambert studied her for a long, uncomfortable moment. "I'm not sure why you would do this," he admitted, "but I will certainly find out. So if you're not being completely honest with me, you need to do so right now."

He actually thought she was making up the story. "I am telling you that Raymond Douglas was here and someone killed him...or at least hurt him. I saw him—his body—being dragged across that kitchen floor, and I saw blood."

This was unbelievable. Frustration joined the mix of anger and outrage.

"I've interviewed by phone three of the five employees who closed up the restaurant tonight," Lambert said. "They all confirmed that Mr. Douglas was fine and intended to leave shortly after they left. In fact, one saw him at the rear exit just before she left the kitchen."

"Wait...what?" How could that be? Those people had let her inside. Why would they leave her in an empty restaurant? Wouldn't they have been suspicious? "That makes no sense at all. Why wouldn't at least one among them have demanded to know why I came into the restaurant? Why would they have allowed me to come inside if no one else was around?"

"That's a question for the manager to pose to his employees." Lambert closed his notepad with a distinct snap. "Since you are not an employee of this establishment, and none of the people to whom I spoke who *are* employees had any idea why you came inside as they were leaving, I can only say that your story feels off somehow. Why would you not ask after Mr. Douglas as the others filed out and you entered? Why would you sit in the dark—basically—for forty-five minutes? You're a bright woman. It seems illogical to me that you would do this."

The idea that he was making far too much sense rattled her.

"I… I don't know what else to say. He asked me out on a date, and I followed his instructions on where and when to meet him. The delay was annoying, but I wanted to be patient." She shrugged. "To tell you the truth, it's been a while since I've been on a date, period, much less basically a blind date. I guess I thought I was giving him the benefit of any doubt."

Again, Lambert considered her for several seconds. "I also called Mr. Douglas's assistant, who confirmed he was scheduled on the red-eye to Los Angeles. We're still attempting to verify that he boarded the plane, but the vacation appears to be legitimate. It's your date we can't seem to verify."

This couldn't be. Why would Raymond ask her out and then do this?

It made no sense. They had talked an hour before she came to the restaurant. Maybe he was scheduled for a vacation starting tomorrow. Who knew? Today, actually, since it was well after midnight. Whatever his plans for today, Raymond Douglas had scheduled a date with her for last night. Her friend Isla could verify this.

"I can't tell you about the plans he'd had for today or any other upcoming days," Leah said, her patience thinning, "but I know his plans for last night. As I've told you twice already, you can verify this with my friend, Isla. Raymond and I were going to an exhibit—"

"So you say," he interrupted. "Your friend has not returned my call. In any event, we will locate Mr. Douglas, and I hope that he is alive and well. Either way, I will be speaking with you again, Ms. Gerard. You are free to go for now. I'll be in contact as soon as I confirm our missing *victim's* whereabouts. Then we'll go from there."

This was so wrong. Leah pushed back her chair and stood. She swayed just a bit. She was tired and totally at the end of her emotional rope. All that aside, she was not some prankster or criminal or whatever this detective thought she was.

"I know what I saw, Detective," she repeated. "Apparently, I can't make you believe me—but when he doesn't show up you'll know I was right."

"If," he said, waylaying her plan of turning her back to him and marching angrily away, "he doesn't show up, I'm afraid your problems will be just beginning, Ms. Gerard."

"Why is that?" What the heck was he insinuating?

"If Mr. Douglas is truly missing and you were the last person in the vicinity of where he was last seen, then that would make you our prime suspect—wouldn't you agree?"

Oh. My. God. This could not be happening. "If I had something to do with his disappearance—injury and probably murder, because I know what I saw—why would I call the police? More importantly," she added, "why would I stay here and wait for them to arrive?"

"Stranger things have happened, Ms. Gerard, believe me. For now, don't leave the city. We will be talking again." He rose from his chair. "Since you walked here, Officer Clayton will take you home." He nodded to the female officer standing by.

Leah almost said she would prefer to walk back home as well, but given the circumstances, she would gladly accept a ride.

No matter what this detective believed, Raymond Douglas was likely dead. Leah firmly believed that someone had murdered him right here in this restaurant.

Surely the police would figure that out when they didn't find him. Knots tied in her belly. But then, Lambert was right: she was the only person left in this restaurant when he vanished.

"This way, Ms. Gerard," Officer Clayton said, breaking into her new nightmare.

Leah followed the other woman, unsure of what else to do. There was one other thing she suddenly understood with utter clarity.

Once the police involvement in whatever happened here tonight got out, the killer—and there was a killer, or kidnapper, or *whatever* out there somewhere—would know someone else besides him and Raymond had been in the restaurant.

How long would it take that person to find Leah?

Chapter Two

Monday, August 11
Gerard/Morris Apartment
Chestnut Street, 9:30 a.m.

Leah parted the slats of the blinds and peeked out the window. Her heart sank. The car was still there. Fear crept up her spine, making her shiver.

That car had been there all night. Two-door sedan, black. She couldn't determine the make. Nothing sporty or particularly sleek. Generic...nondescript.

The first time she had spotted the vehicle was late yesterday, just before dark. After getting home from the nightmare would-be blind date, she had gone straight to bed. Ended up sleeping a good portion of the day away. She hadn't even bothered to call Isla and tell her what happened. Surely the detective had gotten in touch with her by now. Frankly, she was surprised her friend hadn't called her and asked what the heck happened.

Didn't matter. Isla would be home tonight anyway. Leah could tell her everything then. This was not the kind of conversation to have over the phone. It was too bizarre...too personal.

She cradled her mug of coffee, wished the caffeine

would kick in. This was her second cup, and she really, really needed the boost. Detective Lambert would be here at ten. She'd spent hours last night searching for news about Raymond, but she'd found nothing. No mention of him at all, actually. Not a single word about an incident at the Chop House. Did that mean Raymond really was on vacation? She supposed she would find out when the detective arrived. More knots twisted in her belly. On some level, she understood that somehow this was not going to turn out well. The whole situation was far too strange. As much as she wanted to believe there would be a logical—if not reasonable—explanation, she didn't believe that to be true.

She'd already missed a shift at the library, and she'd had no choice but to call out today as well. So much for adding to her savings. But work was the furthest thing from her mind just now. She wanted—no, she *needed* to understand what had happened in that restaurant kitchen. To the man she'd gone there to meet. The idea that she had fallen asleep and somehow dreamed the whole incident was absolutely ludicrous.

The buzzer sounded, warning her that she had a caller at the entrance to the building. Bracing herself, she crossed to the door and picked up the handset of the intercom mounted on the wall.

"Yes?"

"Detective Lambert here for our appointment, Ms. Gerard."

"Come on up." She pressed the button that would release the door lock for the detective. She desperately wished to never see him again, but there was no hope for that until this thing was figured out. Her head still swam with uncertainty each time she replayed the events of last night. A tiny part of her had even started to wonder if she was losing her mind.

No, she saw what she saw. This detective needed to figure out what had happened. That was his job.

Maybe, if she was really lucky, he had news that would clear up this terrible mess. Doubtful, but she could hope. Leah hung up the handset and readied to open the door. Depending on whether he took the elevator or the stairs, he'd be here fairly quickly. The apartment she and Isla shared was on the second floor. It wasn't very large, but it was affordable for two students juggling jobs and student loans to get their educations. She and Isla were the same age, but unlike Leah, her roommate hadn't taken a break before continuing her education. By this time next year, Isla would be moving on from medical school to an internship while Leah would be hoping to land a position teaching English literature at a university. She should have completed her undergrad degree and this master's years ago, but a bad decision she never again wanted to think about had gotten in the way.

A knock on the door made her jump, even though she'd known it was coming.

She checked the view finder. Detective Lambert, shoulders squared and eyes narrowed, stared back at her. She opened the door and propped a smile into place. "Please, come in."

"Thank you for seeing me on such short notice," he said. He stepped inside and surveyed the space.

Leah closed and locked the door. She always did so without thinking, but with the possibility that someone was watching her apartment, she was uncomfortable even with it locked. For a moment she wondered how the detective was sizing up her place. Small, but nice—*nice* meaning well maintained and in a good location. There wasn't much on the walls as far as photos or decor of any sort. Who had the time? The furnishings were a mishmash of what she and Isla had each owned before Leah had moved in. Since their styles were completely different, there was no true theme to the decor. Just a mix of Isla's ultramodern pieces and Leah's slightly more traditional stuff. Actually, the place had looked better—cleaner design-wise—before Leah added her things. The apartment had been Isla's for several years when she and Leah met and became roommates.

She gestured to the living room area. "Have a seat."

Though the detective crossed the room and paused at the sofa, he waited until she settled there to lower into one of the chairs. He chose the traditional overstuffed, upholstered one that belonged to Leah instead of Isla's modular leather-and-chrome one. The sofa and chairs were clustered near the one double window in the room. In Leah's opinion, that rather large window was one of the most important features of the space. She loved that she could watch the people on the sidewalks and the comings and goings on the street whenever she wanted, since they lived in such a vibrant neighborhood.

She really enjoyed living in this city. Hadn't regretted her move here five years ago for a single moment. Well, at least until Saturday night. She had to admit a brief bout with regret after that disturbing event.

"Did you find him?" she asked the man watching her intently. Perhaps that explained the unexpected meeting. She braced herself for bad news.

"Well—" he crossed one leg over the other, settling his ankle atop his knee "—that depends on how you define the word. We did find evidence that he had a vacation planned. At some point before the scheduled flight, he changed it to Sunday afternoon rather than the middle of the night on Saturday, which, for what it's worth, lends some credibility to your story of a date. We also learned that he did not make the flight. His assistant has not heard from him. He has not checked in to the hotel in Los Angeles, and he is not at home. Based on a search of his residence, he had packed for the trip, but his suitcase still sits on the bed."

Regret and dread funneled through her. She had sincerely hoped he would be found on vacation in Los Angeles and would admit that he'd decided to stand her up but hadn't possessed the guts to even send a text. Although she had known better, she had still, deep down, hoped she'd imagined or dreamed the whole thing.

"He *is* missing, then." Of course he was. She had seen him dragged across the floor, blood leaking from his head. He was missing and injured...possibly dead.

"Yes. Raymond Douglas is officially missing. Since there has been no ransom demand, it's unlikely that he's still alive—based on what you allegedly witnessed. Whatever the case, be aware," he warned, "that this information has not been released. The few details we have are not to be shared under any circumstances. I tell you this only because I need your full cooperation."

His last statement hit her the wrong way. "Are you suggesting I haven't been cooperating? For God's sake, I've done everything you asked me to do. I've answered all your questions." *Suffered being made to feel like a fool*, she kept to herself.

He studied her for another long moment. "Tell me about your relationship with Chris Painter," he said, rather than answer her question.

The unexpected change in direction of the discussion was like a dash of cold water in her face. Where the hell had that come from? "What does a personal relationship I had over nine years ago have to do with what happened to Raymond?"

"Maybe nothing," he returned with a half shrug. "But indulging my curiosity is part of cooperating, to my way of thinking."

Her pulse revved up. He was serious. Clearly, he'd been digging around in her past. She shouldn't be surprised, but somehow she was. "What is it that you want to know?"

"The two of you had a bad breakup, and then Painter disappeared," Lambert said. "No one heard from him again. Still haven't, according to the detective I spoke with from your hometown."

A twisted combination of fear and anger swelled inside her. "If you spoke with Detective Hawkins," she began, choosing her words carefully, "then you know that Chris was a drug dealer. A thug. He was in and out of jail, and he made a lot of enemies. When he disappeared, most people believed he crossed the wrong guy and was taken out of play. I was eighteen, naive and wild about a very bad man. My parents tried to tell me that he was serious trouble, but I wouldn't listen. I was convinced I was in love, but I was wrong. That is all I know about the disappearance of Chris Painter."

Humiliation joined the other emotions swarming inside her. As a teenager, she had made a terrible mistake. She'd hurt and disappointed her parents, and she'd been dragged into a long and painful criminal investigation because she had been an immature and foolish girl who acted on impulse and emotion rather than logic and intelligence. Her senior year of high school was not her best by any stretch of the imagination. For the entire rest of her academic days, from kindergarten on, she had been a model student—one who made the very best grades and good choices. But it was that one lone, final year of high school—actually, the last few weeks—for which everyone in her small hometown would remember her. How sad was that?

Lambert nodded. "That's basically what Detective Hawkins said," he admitted. "But you can see how learning this information would give me pause under the circumstances."

She nodded, uncertain of her voice at the moment.

"The circumstances are oddly similar. Don't you agree?"

"Actually, I don't." She managed a tight swallow to dampen her dry throat. "I did not see whatever happened to Chris occur, and it was fairly clear to all who knew him why he vanished. At least, as clear as an unsolved disappearance can be. But this is not the same at all."

When he made no comment, she kept going. "Obviously, you don't believe me when I say I saw Raymond on that floor. His eyes were open and unblinking. Blood was leaking down the side of his head." She gestured to her left temple. "From where I was standing, he looked dead or...maybe unconscious."

Lambert took a long, deep breath, then released it. "I'm

supposed to believe that in the twenty-odd minutes between the time you witnessed his body on the floor and being moved until the first on the scene arrived, someone removed the body from the building and cleaned up any evidence a crime had taken place in that kitchen?"

His doubts were undeniably justified...but she was telling the truth. "It's the *only* explanation because I know what I saw."

Lambert uncrossed his legs and leaned forward, braced his forearms on his knees. "Did you know that Mr. Douglas carried a ten-million-dollar life insurance policy?"

Leah made a face. "Why would I know that? We'd only ever met once." She shook her head. "I can't believe this."

The detective turned up his hands. "It was necessary to ask. Just another worrisome detail to clear up."

"Then the beneficiary on the policy should give you a starting place on who might have reason to want him dead," she suggested. This man was a seasoned detective. She had done a little research on him too. He was good. His name or face was, it seemed, always in the news for solving some case or another. Unquestionably, he was well-versed in how to conduct a criminal investigation. She suspected he only wanted her reaction to the question. Evidently, unsettling the witness was part of his strategy.

"His ex-wife is one of the beneficiaries," Lambert said. "But she has an airtight alibi—she and her two teenage children spent the weekend with her mother."

Leah lifted her chin in defiance of the statement. "Maybe she hired someone to do it. Based on how quickly everything happened that night, it certainly gave the appearance of a professional job. A well-planned one, obviously." As soon as the words were out of her mouth, she wished she could take them back. Knowledge of that sort of thing was not a good look on a suspect. But she was only guilty of watching too much crime TV. And, admittedly, mystery novels were her favorite.

He nodded. "It does."

To her surprise, it practically sounded like he believed her. Leah had told herself not to forget to ask this next question, but she almost had. "What about cameras? Were there no cameras in the alley, or anywhere around the building, that showed the comings and goings at the rear exit of the restaurant?" She found it difficult to believe there weren't, but there had been no mention so far.

"Only one, and it wasn't working at the time."

She should have seen that one coming. "So, what now? Do you have other suspects, or are you determined to try and pin this on me, because I can tell you—" her voice rose with each word "—I did not have anything to do with this. I didn't even know the man."

"Well." He stood. "I'm sure I will have more questions."

Leah stood, too, her knees a little weak. Why couldn't he just give her an answer? Was she still a suspect, given what he'd learned about the insurance policy?

"Did you speak to Isla?"

"Unfortunately, I have not been able to reach her."

Frustration wove its way through Leah, but she wasn't surprised. When Isla was at work at the ER, she oftentimes left her cell phone in her locker. If she was in class, she had no doubt turned it off. Still, she usually returned calls. A new thread of uneasiness trickled through Leah.

"I hope you will contact me if you recall anything else I might need to know."

She followed him to the door, the urge to shake him and somehow make him understand that she was innocent in this a pulsing urge in her body.

Lambert hesitated at the door. "Was there anything else you wanted to tell me?"

She thought of the car. "Yes." She moistened her lips. "There's been a black sedan across the street since last night. There's a man—I think it's a man—inside. I feel like he might be watching me" She shrugged. "I can't help wondering if perhaps I'm in danger."

Concern or something like it materialized in his expression. "Show me the car you mean."

She led the way back to the window and surveyed the street. Frustration sagged her shoulders. The car was gone. "I guess he left."

"Perhaps it was one of ours," he suggested. "We had someone keeping an eye on your apartment the first eight or so hours after you left the restaurant, but not since. It's not impossible there was a miscommunication on the time frame. Still, if you notice anything that makes you feel threatened, call me." He hesitated. "You make a good point about the wife maybe hiring someone to get rid of her husband."

Hope dared to sprout. "Yes," she said with a nod. "It happens in the movies all the time."

"Maybe she hired you to play the part of witness to his murder."

Her jaw dropped, but any potential rebuttal flew out of her head.

With that blatant accusation, he walked away. This time when he reached the door, he opened it and left, calling out a *good day* over his shoulder.

She hurried across the room, locked the door and sagged against it. She was in serious trouble here. Somehow she had believed this would sort itself out, but that wasn't happening. At this point, she would be a real fool not to recognize it was only getting worse. What she needed was an attorney. No, Leah decided... What she needed was someone who could help her figure this out. Maybe even help her find the person responsible for this nightmare.

A private investigator. A good one. A really, really good one.

The Colby Agency, 2:00 p.m.

"Ms. Gerard."

Leah jerked to attention. She'd been a million miles away. "Yes." She stood and produced a smile for the young woman who had called her name. Blond hair, blue eyes, very well put together. Professional pale blue suit.

"I'm Jamie Colby." She extended her hand.

Leah shook her hand, then suffered a fleeting doubt considering how very young the woman appeared to be. Maybe she was an assistant? "Thank you for making time to see me." Leah was so, so grateful to be able to get an appointment today—even if only with an assistant.

"Of course." Jamie gestured to the corridor beyond the lobby. "Walk with me to my office, and we'll figure this out."

Leah strode alongside the other woman as she led the way down a carpeted corridor flanked by doors on either side. The decor was surprisingly elegant—more so than Leah had expected, even though the agency was listed as the top in the business. Somehow the idea of a PI always made her think of shabby offices on the seedy side of town. This was a seriously upscale area and a prestigious building.

Jamie's office was spacious and filled with light. A large window looked out over the street. Maybe not an assistant. The realization that her last name was Colby struck Leah just then. Probably...definitely not an assistant.

After the offer of refreshments, they settled at a small conference table on one side of the well-appointed room.

"You mentioned the Douglas case," Jamie said, kicking off the meeting. "I reached out to my contact at Chicago PD and learned that Detective Anthony Lambert has that one. He has a very good reputation and will go to great lengths to solve the matter."

Leah nodded. "I read about him on the internet. The trouble is, he's so focused on me it feels like he isn't looking at anyone else."

"You are listed as a person of interest," Jamie agreed. "But that's not unusual. Oftentimes an investigation will include a good many persons of interest, and that list will get whittled down as the investigator moves forward, gathering information and evidence." She smiled reassuringly. "It's not personal, just part of the process. So, why don't you walk me through how you're involved?"

Leah didn't hesitate. She launched into the unnerving story, taking care not to leave out a single detail. If this agency was going to help her, she had to ensure they knew everything. It certainly sounded as if they had all the right contacts. Just further proof of the caliber of investigators on staff. In light of Lambert's visit that morning, Leah went ahead and shared the details about Chris Painter.

Though her distant past couldn't possibly have anything to do with this case, Lambert seemed to think otherwise or wanted to give that impression. She was here for help. No one could help her without all the necessary details—even the ugly ones that seemed irrelevant.

"I appreciate your thoroughness," Jamie said. "Based on the situation as we know it at this time, I feel that investigator Owen Walker would be an excellent fit for your case. I've spoken with him at length, so he's aware of the situation. I'd like to introduce you and let the two of you talk, if you're ready to move forward."

Leah nodded. "Yes, please."

She had been informed of the retainer fee and costs during her initial call. As much as Leah hated to part with any of her savings, she had a feeling this was necessary to her survival of whatever was coming. If she'd had any doubts, seeing that black sedan parked outside her building again when she left for this appointment had sealed her decision.

Jamie used the phone on her desk to summon the investigator. Half a minute later the door opened, and he joined the meeting.

Owen Walker was a very attractive man. Tall, broad shouldered. Maybe thirty-two or thirty-three. Isla would swoon. Leah couldn't deny a bit of a swoony reaction herself. She could see him on the cover of a fashion magazine or leading the cast in a television series. Not to mention on a romance novel.

She just hoped his skills were as impressive. The last thing she needed was eye candy.

He introduced himself, shook her hand, but he didn't

take a seat. "I prefer to kick off a relationship with a new client in a less formal setting," he explained.

Nice voice too. Deep, smooth. A charmer. Her failed blind date had been a charmer. Oh God…maybe this had been a mistake.

"There's a coffee shop," he went on. "Just down the block."

Leah pushed to her feet. "Sounds good." She turned to Jamie, who had risen from her seat as well. "Thank you for your time, Jamie." She prayed it wasn't going to be a waste of her own.

"Thank you." She gave Leah a nod. "You can stop worrying now. You're in very good hands."

Leah hoped, hoped, hoped that was true. She had never done anything like this, and she wasn't sure how it worked. She glanced at the man assigned to her case. This was the Colby Agency. The agency had a fantastic reputation. She had to believe this man would be of the highest caliber available in the field. She drew in a deep breath. At least she'd gotten the ball rolling. This thing was getting far too complicated and more than a little scary.

Doing something was better than doing nothing.

As they rode the elevator down to the main lobby, he asked, "How long have you been in Chicago?"

"I moved here five years ago." For four years after the Chris disaster, she had drifted around, never feeling completely comfortable anywhere she landed—from Peoria, where she'd grown up, to Springfield and then up to Rockford and a few places in between, eventually landing in Chicago. Even though she'd spent the first two years in the Windy City juggling school and keeping a low-rent roof over her head, this felt like home for the first time since she'd left Peoria. Maybe it was more about finding her good friend Isla two years after settling in Chicago. "I can't see myself ever leaving."

"It's a dynamic city, for sure," he agreed.

When the elevator stopped, they crossed the grand lobby and exited the building. The afternoon sun had cranked up. This summer had been one for the books so far. Leah was ready for fall.

"What about you?" she asked.

"I'm a transplant. Moved from Miami ten years ago."

"Talk about a climate change."

"A bit different, yes."

He smiled, and it only confirmed her idea that he could certainly grace the covers of magazines and books. Wow.

But could he solve this case?

Deep in her shoulder bag, her phone clanged its vintage ringtone. Even though she'd lowered the volume, it still sounded too loud in the moment.

"Excuse me." With her mother's health deteriorating these days, she was careful never to ignore her phone. She checked the screen. Didn't recognize the number. She frowned, then glanced at the man beside her. "I should probably get this."

He nodded and she tapped the screen. "Hello?"

"Leah, it's Roger Bolling."

The building manager. Her instincts sharpened. "Hey, Roger. Is everything all right?"

"Not really. There was an explosion at your door."

Leah stalled. "What?" She couldn't have heard him right.

"Some guy made a flower delivery. Since you weren't home, he left it outside your door. Five minutes after the guy exited the building, there was an explosion. Blew the door off its hinges and started a fire. Luckily, I was here and got it put out before there was much damage. The fire department is here. Cops too."

"Oh my God, was anyone hurt?"

"No, no. That's the upside. But, as I said, the police are here, and they want to talk to you."

What in the world? Emotions twisted inside her. "I'll be there in fifteen minutes."

Chapter Three

Gerard/Morris Apartment
Chestnut Street, 5:00 p.m.

The wall around the hole that had once been the door to her apartment was blackened by the fire the explosion had caused. The door itself had splintered into numerous pieces and was scattered all over the living area inside the apartment. The odor of smoke lingered in the air, even though the flames had been extinguished almost immediately, before Leah even got the call.

Detective Lambert was already at the scene when they arrived. There were several other uniformed police officers and at least two more in plain clothes like Lambert. The fire department was just preparing to leave, except for the fire marshal; he and Lambert were in deep conversation.

Leah felt numb. This couldn't be happening...and yet, it was.

"Were you expecting flowers from anyone?" her newly hired PI asked.

Leah laughed despite the fact that she felt more like crying. "No. I haven't been sent flowers..." She laughed again, a sad self-deprecating sound, and shook her head. "Ever."

He gave a nod. "I'll talk to Detective Lambert and see what they've learned."

Leah stood several yards away from her apartment, behind a ribbon of yellow crime scene tape. She sagged against the wall. The whole building had been evacuated, and residents were only now being allowed back inside. The neighbors who lived nearest to her eyed her suspiciously as the ribbon was moved aside for each one to pass through. She was the only one who wouldn't be moving beyond this point. The hole that had been her door was draped with two more ribbons of yellow crime scene tape. The ribbon hung like an X over the opening.

She had called Isla and left a message warning her about the explosion. Leah already knew exactly what her friend and roommate would say when she called back: Isla would insist she cared nothing about the personal items they might have lost. She only cared that Leah was safe and unharmed. And she was—physically, anyway. Her mind, however, was reeling. Her emotions were a shipwreck. How on earth had this happened? First the blind date from Hades, and now this!

Who sent a bomb hidden in flowers? There was something so very sadistic about the idea.

Her arms tightened around her torso. How was she supposed to react to all this? To feel? The one thing she sensed with certainty was that she had to find out why this was happening. And where the apparent danger was coming from.

Danger. Why in the world would she be in danger? She had nothing and knew nothing that was overly important or represented a threat to anyone. It was sad to say, but basically she was a nobody.

This could not be her life!

But then again, it wasn't like it hadn't happened before.

She closed her eyes and blocked the memories from nine plus years ago. That had been another life. This one was calm and sedate...boring, even. How could she possibly be relevant enough to anyone or anything to be in danger?

Yet somehow she felt exactly like one of the informants in a crime movie, where the bad guys were doing everything possible to stop her and the good guys weren't sure they could trust her.

It was the most bizarre situation. Leah had done nothing wrong. She'd agreed to a date. A sort of odd one, to be sure—to meet someone at half an hour before midnight and wait in a closed, dimly lit dining room while he handled a bit of business. In hindsight, the whole plan was the very picture of a scene from a gangster novel. Why had she not considered the oddity of it all before agreeing? Was she that desperate?

No, Isla had been that desperate for her. Leah had never been the pushy type. Nevertheless, she appeared to be drawn to that very personality type. She was the one who went along. Her life was busy enough without shoehorning social activities into it. But her friends—Isla, in particular—had insisted she needed to get out more. One thing was certain: This was the last time she would agree to a blind date. Ever.

The next time she agreed to spend time with a potential boyfriend—assuming she wasn't dead or in prison after this—she would set the terms. And she would do her homework. Her frustration wasn't aimed at Raymond—not really. He had seemed like a perfectly nice guy. It was difficult to hold a grudge against a man who could very well have been murdered.

Don't even go there, Leah. At this point, she had no idea what had happened to him. Kidnapped? Murdered? She shuddered.

As if her thoughts had summoned the two of them, Owen Walker and Detective Lambert started toward her. Her anxiety crept up a notch.

Just stay calm and tell the truth.

But that was what she had been doing, and look where that had gotten her. She stared at the hole of a door to her apartment, and her shoulders slumped.

Whatever else happened, and whatever it meant, the truth was all she had. The many and varied possible unknowns made her feel cold and alone. Who would do this to her? When she and Owen had arrived at her building, she'd been fairly certain she spotted the black sedan. With all the worries about the explosion, she hadn't mentioned it. There was no time to agonize over whether she was being paranoid.

There were bigger issues.

Who would send her flowers? More importantly, who would send her flowers with a bomb inside? This truly was so far over-the-top that she couldn't even see it, much less begin to understand it.

But it was happening...*to her*.

"Mr. Walker tells me you have no idea who would have sent you flowers," Lambert said as he came to a stop next to her.

"None." She shrugged. "I mean, I never get flowers."

Never had, but there was no need to repeat that sad fact. Owen had likely already told the detective as much.

"The building has security cameras," Lambert said. "We were able to see the delivery person stopping the van on the street and bringing the flowers inside, then him exiting the building. Unfortunately, he wore a baseball cap with the bill pulled low, shadowing his face. He seemed quite aware of the security cameras. There were no markings on the van, on his clothing. He may have been a hired driver and had no idea there was a bomb."

Just like last night...except this time the results of the incident were undeniable.

"What do I do now?" She glanced once more at what remained of her apartment. "I understand I can't stay here, but how in the world will you figure out who is doing this and why? It all started with what happened at the restaurant, and I am quite honestly completely at a loss as to what to expect next." She hated that she sounded as if she was at the end of her rope, and she hated even worse that tears were burning her eyes. If she cried now, she would just crumple into a heap on the floor.

Keep it together, Leah.

"These things take time," Lambert said. "Fortunately, the quick reaction time of the building manager, Mr. Bolling, prevented any real damage beyond the door. Even so, you and your roommate cannot go into the apartment until the forensic work is done. I'm sure Mr. Bolling will have the door repaired as quickly as possible. But for now, if there are items you need from your room, one of my officers can pack a few things for you."

Leah nodded. "That would be very helpful. Thank you."

She'd wanted to complain. To demand why she was being cast out of her home because someone else had decided to do a bad thing. But it wouldn't change the situation. There were rules, and she had to obey. This whole episode—the past thirty-odd hours—had been mind-boggling. She kept expecting to wake up and realize it was just a bad dream.

Detective Lambert went to one of the uniformed officers and spoke quietly to her before returning to his conversation with the fire marshal. Then Officer Brant—a woman, thankfully—took notes on her cell phone of what items Leah needed and where they could be found in her bedroom. Once Leah had told her everything she could think of, Brant moved the crime scene tape aside and disappeared into the apartment.

"I've spoken with Victoria," Owen said. "I'm to take you to one of our safe houses until we figure this out—if that's okay with you."

A safe house. Dear God, she really *was* in a movie... only this one was far too real.

Leah attempted to work up a smile, but the effort felt entirely miserable. "Thank you. I am so grateful I found the Colby Agency and had the good sense to make that call. Jamie was incredibly helpful."

"She's pretty amazing," Owen agreed. "She's Victoria's granddaughter. You may or may not have read the About section on the website, but Victoria is the one who calls the shots."

"I did, and I also read several articles about Victoria. Her life story is astonishing." Leah wondered how a person—a mother whose son was abducted when he was seven years old, then suddenly returned twenty years later with the single goal of killing her—could survive such an ordeal. She couldn't imagine the strength and fortitude Victoria must possess.

"Then you appreciate that one of her top priorities is protecting those who need it most. We will keep you safe, Leah, until this is done."

She smiled, and this time it was real. "Well, maybe I'll actually sleep tonight. Between worrying about what happened to Raymond Douglas and the person in the black car watching my apartment, I barely slept at all last night."

"There's been someone watching your apartment?" Concern flashed in the investigator's eyes.

"I first noticed it late yesterday, and it was here this morning. When I told Detective Lambert about it—during his visit this morning—we checked, and the car was gone. But I think I saw it when we arrived here a little while ago."

His jaw tightened. "We'll have a look when we leave, after the officer returns with your bag."

Thankfully, the officer ducked under the yellow tape just then, Leah's overnight bag in hand, and made her way toward them.

"Found everything you asked for," Brant said. "You gave very good directions on where to find what you wanted. I wish my bedroom was so orderly."

"I'm a little obsessed with organization," Leah admitted. Disorganization was a pet peeve of hers. The first thing she and Isla had agreed upon when she had asked Leah to share the apartment was the necessity of organization. They were both a little overenthusiastic when it came to everything being in its place. But living in such a small place essentially demanded it.

"Nothing wrong with that," Brant said with a smile.

When the officer had gone on her way, Owen said, "I'll check with Lambert and make sure we're clear to go."

While he walked to the other end of the corridor where Lambert and the fire marshal remained in deep conversation, Leah remembered that she'd forgotten her cell phone charging cord. Oh well, she'd just have to pick one up on the way to the safe house. She wasn't asking the officer to go back into the apartment.

A safe house. She would be staying in a safe house. How in the world had this happened? Didn't matter how many times she asked that question, the answer was always the same: she had no idea.

When Owen returned, he nodded. "We can leave now."

As grateful as she was to be leaving, the lingering smell of smoke and the realization of what had happened were ramping up her anxiety. She couldn't help feeling just a little terrified at the prospect of what might happen next. She'd seen lots of safe houses in the movies and in television shows, but she'd never expected to be staying in one herself. How long would she be expected to stay there? Would there be additional costs? Her budget couldn't take many more surprises.

Outside, she scanned the street for the black sedan. Like before, when she wanted to show someone she wasn't imagining things, it was nowhere to be seen. But it had been there when they arrived, she was certain of it.

"I saw it," she said, suddenly feeling defensive. She realized how she sounded but, damn it, this was ridiculous.

"I'm sure you did," Owen said. "Unless the driver already saw what he needed to see or found what he needed to find, the one thing you can count on is that he or she will be back. We will catch him."

His words relaxed her just a little. Her shoulders loosened, and drawing in a breath came easier. "I like that plan."

He opened the passenger-side door of his sporty silver car and waited for her to settle in. Once he'd closed the door, he moved around to the driver's side and slid behind the wheel.

"Where is the safe house?" She sank deeply into the luxurious leather seats and relaxed a bit more.

"This one's on Elm Street. It's great. You'll see."

Colby Agency Safe House
East Elm Street, 6:50 p.m.

HE WASN'T WRONG when he said it was great.

Leah wasn't sure how she would prevent her jaw from perpetually dropping. The safe house was an 1879 brownstone in the fabled historic area of East Elm. The place was truly gorgeous.

Just walking up the steps was awe inspiring. The architecture was splendid. Inside, things only got better. The ceilings soared, and the historic details had been carefully maintained while, at the same time, modernizing as needed. The windows were large and allowed a tremendous amount of natural light to flood into the rooms. Beautifully maintained hardwoods and a staircase that made you want to climb up to the next floor, your fingers trailing the intricately carved railing as you went. There were fireplaces in every room, her host explained. All restored so meticulously. The pièce de résistance was an intimate courtyard in the back that was completely self-contained with trees and shrubs, making it at once welcoming and utterly private. It was like being in a natural refuge miles from the city, and yet it was right here in the heart of Chicago.

"Wow, this is incredible. Like a vacation in a perfectly splendid VRBO."

"The agency has safe houses all over. Some in town, some miles away. This one allows us to be close to the ongoing investigation and yet securely away from any trouble. Your privacy and security are our top priority."

"And I appreciate it more than you can possibly know." Well, if this investigation was going to test her sanity and her safety as well as decimate her finances, at least she would be living in luxury.

"I'll take your bag to your room, and then we can see what's in the kitchen."

He'd insisted on carrying her bag from her building to the car and then into the brownstone. She imagined he was a real gentleman even when he wasn't on the job. Owen Walker gave every impression of being a really nice man.

"Should I come along?"

He smiled and indicated that she should go first. "Of course. You can pick your room instead of me selecting it for you, if you'd like."

"I imagine all the rooms are lovely," she said as they climbed the stairs.

"They are. You'll only need to decide if you want a street view or a lake view."

"I think I'll go with the lake view." Maybe the water would calm her nerves. She could use a little serenity right now.

"Very good choice." He flashed her another one of those smiles that made her smile back without thinking.

A new worry nudged her. This part of her current reality was suddenly feeling far too good to be true. When would the other shoe drop? She banished the thought. Clearing those haunting *what-if*s from her head was the only way to hang on to some semblance of peace of mind.

The room with the best lake view was on the third floor, according to her host. The large window turned out to be French doors that opened onto a small balcony. And like he said, the view from that balcony was utterly breathtaking.

"What about you?" She turned to her host. "Where will you be sleeping?"

The notion that she would love to hear him say "with you" flashed through her sleep-deprived mind.

Not smart, Leah.

"I'll be on the second floor, just below you. No one is getting to you without going through me first."

If he'd meant to make her feel safe, he'd done a fantastic job. "That definitely makes me feel better."

He deposited her bag onto the four-poster bed. "Now, let's see what we can scrounge up for dinner."

She didn't mention that ramen noodles were a mainstay at her place. Owen didn't look like an instant-meal kind of guy.

Leah loved how the staircase spiraled through the brownstone from the first floor to the top. She could glance over the railing and see all the way to the entry hall. It was so lovely. It really was like taking a vacation without ever leaving the city. Isla would be jealous. They often talked about getaways in some beautiful European city. Isla was likely the one who would eventually be able to afford an international vacation.

But this was pretty close...sort of.

The kitchen appeared to have original cabinetry—or at least something similar. But after opening a few doors and a few drawers, Leah recognized they were new, state of the art. The appliances were as well, but somehow the designer had found a way to bring it all together, as if every aspect was original and belonged exactly where it was, even though the house was more than a century old. There was even a hidden microwave and pantry. An island that looked like an old butcher's table from a shop that once sold select meats hand-carved right in front of the customer stood in the middle of the generous room. Though the island looked vintage, it was complete with at least one electrical outlet and a beautiful light fixture hanging above it.

"As you can see—" Owen pointed to the interior of the massive fridge "—the menu is quite extensive. We can throw together any number of entrees."

He was right about that. Someone had stocked the fridge with a wide variety of goodies. She spotted the ready-to-bake pizza from her favorite local artisan shop. The pizzas were prepared fresh every day.

"Someone must have known I love Giovanni's pizza." She didn't even care if it was veggie or meat lovers; the crust was to die for. Everything else was just icing on the cake.

"Pizza it is, then." He reached for the package.

She scanned the contents of the fridge once more. "I can put together a salad."

"Perfect." Another heart-stopping smile flashed at her.

As he headed for the range, another worry poked into her head. This spending 24/7 together might not be as simple as she'd first thought. At least not until she got her mind off his smile and his...other assets. The primary problem was, she'd been dateless for far too long.

Salad, she told herself. *Focus on prepping the salad.*

She moved the ingredients to the island and then searched for bowls. "There is a variety of dressings. Which would you prefer?" Small talk was good. Kept her from overthinking.

"Surprise me." He glanced over his shoulder. "Truth is, I like them all."

Handsome and easy to please. "You got it."

The next few minutes were filled with sounds of the flames in the gas oven roaring to life and the chopping or tearing of veggies until the two bowls she had selected were brimming with lush salad. She took two plates to the dining table, then the necessary silverware and the bowls of salad.

"Wine?" she asked as she reentered the kitchen.

He pointed to the end of the kitchen where the back door was located. "The wine cabinet and fridge are in those cabinets."

The doors that she had thought belonged to the pantry actually opened to a sort of wine bar. The overhead crisscross shelves held a wide selection to choose from. Below were two counter-height wine fridges that were also well stocked. Since the pizza had a little bit of everything in the way of toppings, she selected a prosecco. With the bottle tucked under one arm, she claimed a couple of wineglasses and carried everything to the dining table.

By the time she had located the linen napkins and arranged the settings, Owen arrived with the pizza.

They settled around the table, and he served the pizza and poured the wine. For a few minutes they enjoyed the meal. Leah hadn't realized she was ravenous until she smelled the pizza baking. She had missed lunch entirely. Breakfast had been a protein bar nearing its expiration date.

It was possible she would be embarrassing herself in the next few minutes because she was starving. Just as she had anticipated, the pizza was amazing. She'd done pretty well with the salad too.

After they'd eaten for a while, he said, "Tell me about the boyfriend who disappeared when you were eighteen."

Leah dabbed her lips with the napkin. She'd expected the subject to come up eventually. "Like I told Detective Lambert—"

He held up a hand. "Don't tell me what you told Lambert. Tell me how it was for you. The facts are one thing, the impact another."

Her face flushed a little. She hadn't expected him to pinpoint the difference so precisely. "All right. I was young. My parents were intensely strict. Religious, but not overly so. Just strict. They wanted their only child—me—to make good choices. To grow up and do important things. Their way of making sure that happened was keeping me under their thumb."

"To protect you." He sipped his wine, his blue eyes watching her intently.

He had the bluest eyes. "Yes."

A moment passed, and then she went on. "I was at the Stop-N-Go, grabbing a soft drink after school. I was two weeks away from graduating, and I could not wait to get out of Peoria. I was humming with the need to be on my own—to be free! Chris came in to pay for gas, and I was infatuated instantly. The way he talked...the way he walked...everything about him screamed *wicked*, and he was very handsome. I was a kid, and that was all I saw. He must have noticed me gawking, because he started flirting. The next thing I knew, I was giving him my cell number and that was that. I was hooked." She shook her head. "I had no idea what he really was. My parents tried to tell me, but I wouldn't listen. He was all I thought about. I spent that entire summer hanging on his every word and deed. My poor parents were both horrified and terrified."

"How did the summer end?"

He asked the question so quietly, but there would be nothing quiet about the answer. The noise and the trauma that answer contained was deeply disturbing. It was the nightmare her parents had worried about.

"Everyone who knew my family understood what my parents were going through in an effort to keep their good girl from going bad. So when Chris disappeared, the community thought my father had killed him. And not a single one blamed him." She shook her head, bit her bottom lip in an effort to stem the tears that rose instantly. "My father was the kindest, gentlest man you would ever meet. The idea that he would harm another soul was ludicrous, and yet, even the police were certain he'd killed Chris and buried him somewhere. The investigation was sheer misery. The way this one detective—not Hawkins, but the one before him—grilled and pushed my father...it was awful."

"But the case was never solved."

Another shake of her head. "Hawkins dug up enough details about Chris's *colleagues* in the drug business to take the heat off my father, but the damage was done. Not to his reputation, mind you. To his health. He suffered a fatal heart attack." She fell silent for a long moment, let the hurt trudge through her. "It was my fault. My mother insisted that was not the case, that heart problems ran in his family, but she knew." Leah nodded, losing the battle with the tears. "I could see it in her eyes no matter what her words said. I killed him."

"I'm certain that was a very difficult time for you and your mother."

"Yeah, well, stupid is as stupid does, and I was stupid. I spent the next four years drifting around trying to find myself, but what I was really looking for was forgiveness… peace. Something along those lines. Sadly, there was no finding it anywhere but in here." She pressed her hand to her chest. "I can't say that I've completely forgiven myself, but I've learned to live with it, and I've taken care of my mother the way my father would have wanted."

As her mother's health had deteriorated in recent years, Leah had made sure she was in the right assisted-living facility and saw the best doctors. Every single dime in the trust her father had left her had gone to making sure her mother was comfortable and as happy as she could be without him. Her mother wasn't pleased with the decision Leah had made, but she had relented when it became clear her daughter wasn't changing her mind. She would be fine. She would be an English professor the way her father was, and she would be a good person. She didn't need the money her father had so carefully saved. She didn't deserve it.

When she was young, Leah and her father would read endlessly and dissect the great classic novels together. To this day, she cherished those memories. If only she hadn't made the mistake of her life. No amount of wishing and using her trust to take care of her mother could fix what she had done.

She could only do her best at being the person her father had believed she could be. It was her singular goal now—besides taking care of her mother. She would be the person he had hoped she would be.

And maybe, just maybe, one day she would be able to forgive herself.

"Tell me about your friend Isla," Owen said then, dragging her from the painful thoughts.

"She's wonderful." A smile tilted Leah's lips, and the tears receded. "She's like the sister I never had. She would do anything for me, and I would do the same for her." She laughed sofly. "Sometimes I can't believe how lucky I was to find a friend like Isla. We really are like sisters."

"The two of you know each other's histories. Like what happened when you were eighteen?"

"We know everything about each other." Leah nodded. She and Isla had no secrets.

"She is the one who introduced you to Raymond Douglas."

"She is. She hadn't seen him in a while, but she had a friend, Maya Ortiz, who served as a sous-chef at the Chop House back in the spring. Maya said Raymond was recently divorced and back in the field. She, Maya and I were at one of our favorite clubs one night a couple of weeks ago and ran into Raymond. I thought for sure Isla was interested in him, but that wasn't the case. She felt he and I would make a good match and..." Leah shrugged. "You know the rest."

"Have you seen Isla or spoken to her since the incident in the restaurant?"

Incident. That was a good way to put it. It was a murder, in Leah's opinion—kidnapping, at the very least—but they had no body, no murder weapon and no evidence of any crime at this point.

She thought about his question. Glanced at the clock on the wall. It was 8:15 p.m., and Isla hadn't called her back about the explosion. "No," she said, frowning.

What could have prevented her friend from calling after receiving the message about the explosion in their apartment and Raymond's disappearance? Until right this moment, Leah had assumed her friend had been busy... but they were beyond that now. This wasn't right. Isla never went this long without letting Leah know what was going on.

"I would have expected her to call by now, but I'm sure something came up and she'll call as soon as she can."

"Have you considered," he ventured, "that Isla could be involved in what happened? Maybe the flowers were for her...rather than for you."

Leah blinked. Made a face. No...that wasn't possible. She and Isla talked about everything. She would never hide anything like that from Leah, and she certainly would not leave her to deal with all this alone. It had to be something major to keep her away...something at work, Leah decided.

"No." She gave her head a hard shake. "Isla wouldn't..."

That's impossible. We tell each other everything." No way. The very notion was impossible.
   Wasn't it?

Chapter Four

Tuesday, August 12
Colby Agency Safe House
East Elm Street, 7:30 a.m.

Leah stood on the small balcony, enjoying the pleasant view and the morning air. She could stand here for hours. Maybe that would help her mind relax and stop spinning.

Isla still hadn't called, and Leah had left her another voicemail.

Something was wrong. Very wrong. She and Isla hadn't been out of contact for this long since their friendship began three years ago.

Isla was in the final weeks of her first year of medical school and working part-time at the Northwestern Memorial ER. Leah had just gotten the job at the library. Her first two years in Chicago, she'd been thankful for her job as a barista at a corner coffee shop near her very modest studio. Another one of Isla's friends had frequented that same library for the workshops. Often, that friend would drag Isla along with her and the two would go for a drink or dinner afterward. On one of those occasions, Isla had invited Leah to join the two of them. She and Isla had become close friends very quickly. The instant Isla found out where Leah lived, she insisted on having her move in with her. It was true that the other neighborhood wasn't the best, but Leah hadn't minded. She was spending all her time at work or at school, so she never really had time to notice. Still, the prospect of moving into Isla's much nicer apartment in such a great neighborhood had been an offer too good to turn down.

From that point forward, they shared everything.

Isla wouldn't just vanish without saying anything unless something was very wrong.

She certainly wouldn't have anything to do with whatever happened to Raymond. Isla was going to be a doctor. She was in her final year of med school, for God's sake. Why would she throw it all away at this stage, when she was so near the finish line?

The concept made no sense at all.

Leah exhaled a big breath and did what she had to do. She couldn't put off any longer going downstairs and facing whatever music fate planned to play for her today. Somehow she would get through it.

She checked her phone once more in the hope that she'd somehow missed the alert indicating Isla had sent a text message or left a voicemail. Nothing from her friend. Nothing from anyone, not even Detective Lambert—the latter actually being a relief. Leah exhaled a big breath and tucked her phone into the back pocket of her jeans. Thankfully, there were extra charging bases and cords here, so she was able to plug up her phone last night without the added trouble of stopping for a new accessory. This safe house came with everything, apparently.

She closed the French doors and walked through the bedroom. The bed had been so comfortable, and still she'd hardly slept. How could she, with all the questions and worries whirling in her head? How had her life become this series of out-of-control elements so quickly?

She glanced at herself in the mirror as she passed the dresser. An elastic she'd forgotten about had been hiding in the bottom of her purse, so it was a ponytail day. She'd tucked her plain white T-shirt into her jeans and donned her favorite sneakers. After all that had happened, she decided casual was the theme until this was done. Worrying about fashion or makeup or any of those usual everyday issues was out the window.

This was way bigger than all those petty concerns.

Her fingers slipped along the sleek railing as she descended the stairs. Such a beautiful old house. She would love to own a brownstone or greystone one of these days—a pipe dream, of course. Her father would say the architecture was befitting an English lit professor. A smile tugged at her lips for a moment before the memory of that devastating loss intruded.

She would get through this, and she would make her father proud. Coming this far had been much too hard to allow anything to get in her way now.

Funny, she mused, if she'd just kept her head down and focused on work and her education, she wouldn't be in this predicament. Evidently, her ability to choose relationship material—or even date material—was seriously lacking.

But then, she hadn't actually done the choosing, had she? She'd allowed her friends to talk her into this one.

Still, it was her decision, ultimately. There was no one to blame except herself.

Isla would never have suggested Raymond Douglas if she'd suspected for a moment he was involved with bad people. She hadn't seen him in ages herself. Perhaps he had changed since she'd known him before. Maybe the trouble that had found him in that restaurant kitchen was part of the reason he was now divorced.

People changed, and sometimes not for the better.

When she was at the bottom of the stairs, the smell of freshly brewed coffee drew her to the kitchen. But it was the basket of muffins and scones on the island that had her mouth really watering.

"Good morning." Owen lifted his mug of coffee in a salute. "I hope you slept well."

"Good morning." Leah picked up a scone and bit into it. Warm, fruity—orange and cranberry—and so, so good. She chewed, moaned. "Did you bake these?" She licked her lips. "If you did, I might just have to keep you forever."

He chuckled. Shook his head.

It was at that exact moment she realized how her comment sounded. "I mean, they're just so good." She took another bite to prevent having to say more and putting her foot further into her mouth.

"I laugh," he explained, "because the idea that I baked anything other than ready-made pizza is funnier than you know. I'm great with simple stuff, but not so much with real baking—or cooking, for that matter. I had the basket delivered by a favorite bakery of mine."

She relaxed, grateful that he wasn't completely perfect. "This scone is to die for."

He smiled. "I'm glad. I wasn't sure if you were a protein-only breakfast person. Or maybe all egg whites and guacamole toast or something like that."

Leah was the one laughing now. "Hardly. That would

be Isla. She is the clean eater. I just eat what I like, even if it isn't good for me."

The mention of her friend's name turned the delicious bite of scone to sand in her mouth.

"I take it she hasn't contacted you."

Leah shook her head. "I'm really worried at this point. This is not like her at all."

"Have you met her family? Do they live in the area?"

"Arlington Heights. And yes, I've been to dinner with her mother many times. Her father was never in the picture. She does have a brother, but he lives in New York. I could call him to see if he's heard from her. He's much older than Isla, so they aren't really close."

Owen considered the information, then suggested, "I think a cold call to the mother would be the most helpful route."

"I was thinking the same thing." Leah abandoned the remainder of her scone to make herself a cup of coffee. She added a little cream and savored the smooth taste. Then she returned to the island and finished off the scone. When she'd devoured the last crumb, she realized he was watching her. She swallowed, grabbed her cup with both hands and took a sip.

"Before we get going this morning," he said, "I wanted to explain that your participation in the investigation is optional—entirely up to you. If you'd like, you can stay here. Catch up on your reading or just relax. It's not necessary for you to be involved in the legwork."

She hesitated a moment before responding. The option of just relaxing was appealing, no question, but she couldn't do it. She had to be part of this. This was her life. Her friend could be in trouble. She couldn't sit around and just wait to see what happened. Not as long as she had a choice, anyway.

"I would prefer to be involved." She really hoped he wasn't going to be disappointed by her answer. She needed to do this.

His lips quirked in a small smile. "I expected as much, but I had to make the offer."

Relief rushed through her. "Since I'm going to be working rather than relaxing, I think I need another scone for fuel." She shot him a look. "Don't judge."

He gave another deep chuckle. "I had two of those large muffins myself. Fuel is a good thing. And for the record, I never judge."

Handsome and kind too. Sigh. Why was it she'd never run into a guy like him before?

A mental eye roll followed the thought. Because she'd kept her head down and her attention on work since pulling her act together five years ago. Prior to that, her decisions had been a little hit or miss, as far as making good ones was concerned. In truth, she was really rusty in the dating field. Her instincts weren't so keen.

Rather than continue to berate herself, Leah concentrated on her coffee, nibbled on that second scone. Then she shared some additional information she'd remembered while she lay *not* sleeping last night. "Isla told me that Raymond has a mother in an assisted-living facility, and she wondered sometimes if the reason he was divorced was because he spent too much time catering to her. Apparently, there was some discontent related to the mother in his marriage. We could talk to his mother, if you think it might be helpful."

"According to the extensive background search done by

the agency—I received a copy of it early this morning—his mother has advanced Alzheimer's. She's in a very upscale facility, and I have my doubts as to whether we would be allowed a visit, or if she would be able to help if we were."

Well, there went that theory.

Again, Leah considered how much she appreciated having the Colby Agency on her side. She had a feeling that finding her friend, the real story about Raymond and her way out of this depended on the man watching her right now.

Morris Residence
Patton Avenue
Arlington Heights, 10:00 a.m.

OWEN PARKED AT the curb in front of the Morris home. The house was small, more a cottage, with an equally small yard filled with blooming shrubs and flowers.

"Her car is home," Leah said.

Owen watched the woman in the passenger seat for a few seconds. Leah Gerard was worried. Understandably so. Her life had been turned upside down with this business. He'd done his research, and Raymond Douglas wasn't quite the upstanding businessman Leah had been led to believe. He'd spent some time as a chef but then realized there was far more money to be made in investments. With that in mind, he'd used his knowledge of Chicago's culinary world to get in on the best and biggest options. In the past five years, his financial worth had skyrocketed. The agency was looking into the possibility of such a huge change in status when his only assets were in the restaurant business. Owen wasn't convinced his new net worth matched his investments.

As well, Leah's friend Isla had a vaguely troubling background as well. Five years ago, there was a brief stint in a private mental hospital. A few months later, a disappearance that was reported to the police and then, only a week later, withdrawn and the case closed. Both parties hid these discrepancies well, but a solid background check and a little extra digging told the tale. Douglas's history showed indications of being a possible scam artist. Morris's reflected a brief period of instability and then nothing but smooth sailing. The real question for Owen was, how did whatever was going on with those two affect or involve Leah—or each other, for that matter?

There were some aspects of the situation that Leah needed to see and learn for herself. It would make accepting how badly she had been fooled somewhat easier. For her sake, he wished there would be better news, that perhaps things weren't as bad as they looked, but he doubted that would prove the case.

Owen had shared the information with Detective Lambert on a phone call that morning. Lambert had been on the right track, but his resources weren't what the Colby Agency's were. He was grateful for the assist. In Owen's opinion, the sooner Leah was cleared of any wrongdoing, the better.

His read on Leah Gerard assured him she was telling the truth about Isla Morris and Raymond Douglas to the best of her knowledge. Not that she was naive; she simply took people at face value until she saw otherwise. There was nothing wrong with that approach, except it did make her susceptible to particularly cunning people.

He had a feeling Douglas was a very experienced player. Morris perhaps more so, in hiding secrets. There was no solid proof of wrongdoing in their known histories, but there were all the earmarks that Owen had instantly recognized: A lack of true friends. Lots of acquaintances but few who were really close. Little or no acknowledged family. In Douglas's case, there was undocumented work and discrepancies in school history.

"Did I pass?"

He frowned, zeroed in on the woman in the passenger seat. She stared at him expectantly. "Pass what?"

It was always easier to mine for more information with a question rather than an answer. Just a little technique he'd picked up during his tenure at the Colby Agency.

"I don't know." She stared out the windshield then. "The way you were staring at me just now made me wonder if you were trying to decide if you trusted me."

"Why wouldn't I?"

"I don't think Detective Lambert believes my story." After a five-second lapse, she turned back to Owen. "Maybe you don't, either, but you just haven't told me."

"Well—" he shut off the engine "—I have found no reason not to believe your story."

"So you've looked," she countered. "Into my background."

"I have. It's necessary to find and consider all that the police will be studying." He offered a reassuring smile. "But don't worry, you have a very good record, save for that brief period related to Painter. Even then, it was only your involvement with bad characters that reflected poorly on you. So you can rest easy. There is no evidence whatsoever that you are not the person you purport to be."

"But I was a terrible person." She looked him directly in the eyes. "I caused my father's death, and that was very bad."

"We all have our own way of looking at ourselves, our individual scale of standards. Some of us set unreasonable expectations for what we can do or did. Some too easily accept blame for the actions of others. It's part of what makes us who we are. You, Leah Gerard, are a good person who made a foolish mistake at a very young age. What you have now is a big problem looming over you like a dark cloud. We're going to alleviate that problem, and we're going to start right now."

She nodded, her eyes a little bright, and reached for the door.

They walked side by side to the front door of the small cottage. Since there was no doorbell, Owen knocked. Two more knocks were required before a voice called out, "Coming."

Leah's relief was palpable. Owen flashed her a smile to reassure her. All they had to do was ask the right questions of the right people, and they would find the answers they needed. That was always the most direct route to resolving a case.

The door opened and a petite woman with gray hair and keen brown eyes looked from Owen to Leah. "Leah! How nice to see you." She instantly drew Leah in for a hug. "You should have called." She patted her loose shoulder-length hair. "I would have prepared myself for visitors."

"You look wonderful as always," Leah insisted. She glanced from Mrs. Morris to Owen and back. "This is my friend Owen, and we're looking for Isla. Have you spoken to her since Saturday?"

A frown marred the older woman's features. "I haven't, and I've been worried." She offered a smile for Owen before shifting her attention back to Leah. "Please, come in. Would you care for some coffee or tea?"

"No thank you," Leah said.

"None for me, thank you," Owen echoed.

Mrs. Morris ushered them inside, closed the door and then took a seat. The door opened right into the small living room. It was a cozy space with lots of clutter—"collections," the lady of the house would likely call them. Bells, little statues of animals.

"Sit wherever you'd like," she insisted.

Owen chose a side chair while Leah settled on the sofa with her friend's mother. His goal during this visit was to watch the older woman closely for any tell that she might be holding back or not speaking the whole truth.

"I'm so worried about her," Leah said. "She never ignores my calls or texts. Do you think something happened with her work at the hospital?"

According to Leah, Isla worked part-time at Northwestern Memorial ER. The background search confirmed as such. She'd moved to that job four years ago, leaving Mount Sinai. It was possible she'd had to work double shifts, but this was well beyond those hours. Only a crisis would keep her there for going on seventy-two hours. The hospital was on his list of places to potentially visit today.

"She hasn't called me back either," Mrs. Morris said, her face pained. "She's supposed to have lunch with me today, but I haven't heard from her."

Leah looked to Owen. "This isn't like Isla at all."

"It is not," Mrs. Morris confirmed. "She is always on time. Never misses an appointment. Really, I'm not just saying that because she's my daughter. This truly is most unusual."

Owen pulled out his cell phone and showed her a picture of Raymond Douglas. "Have you ever seen this man?"

Mrs. Morris took the phone and studied the image. "I don't think so." She frowned, shook her head slowly. "Is he a friend of Isla's?" She passed the phone back to him.

If she recognized Douglas, she hid it well. Owen deferred to Leah for the answer to the woman's question.

"Isla told me she and Raymond—that's the man in the photo—have been friends for years," Leah explained. "She orchestrated a blind date for me with him."

Mrs. Morris's brow furrowed in concentration, as if she were trying to recall the name. "Perhaps he's someone she knows from the hospital or school."

"Perhaps," Leah agreed.

She knew this was not the case, but Owen understood there was no reason to upset Isla's mother further. Owen inquired, "Mrs. Morris, did Isla mention any trips she intended to take or issues she needed to resolve?"

Mrs. Morris searched Owen's face for a long moment, her own clouding with increased worry. "Are you suggesting my daughter is missing or is in some sort of trouble?"

He considered how to answer for a moment. Leah's eyes had widened with uncertainty. She didn't want to upset her friend's mother, which was understandable. But this woman—this mother—was not naive. She knew something was not as it should be.

"There was an incident late Saturday night at the restaurant where Leah was to meet Raymond Douglas for the date Isla had arranged. No one has seen Raymond or Isla since—at least, no one we've found."

"Oh no." Mrs. Morris pressed a hand to her chest. "Should we call the police?"

"The police are already involved with the Douglas case," Owen explained. "We're only just learning that Isla hasn't been returning calls either." He leaned forward, braced his elbows on his spread knees. "So you can see how it's very important that you let Leah know if you hear from Isla or if you have any idea where she might go to get away from the stress of school or work or a boyfriend. The sooner we can confirm her safety and her whereabouts, the better for all concerned."

Mrs. Morris blinked several times, the emotion in her eyes visibly threatening her control. "I will certainly let you know," she said to Leah. "I know Isla adores you, and whatever is going on, she would want you to know."

"I would really appreciate it," Leah told her.

The older woman drew in a big breath. "Some years back, I bought a lake house," she said, this time to Owen. "I haven't been there in a very long time. I actually bought it because the man I was dating at the time loved going to the lake. Ridiculously, I thought we had a future together. Anyway, Isla goes there occasionally." She turned to Leah. "Isla mentioned the two of you going several times. She always enjoyed telling me about your adventures. She said you were too afraid to swim in the lake. That you preferred soaking up the sun on the dock."

Leah's tight smile and vague nod warned there was something off with the story.

"Why don't you give me the address," Owen said,

drawing Mrs. Morris's attention to himself. "Leah and I will go out there and see if Isla is perhaps taking a break from the world. She's done that before, I believe."

"She has," the woman agreed. "She went through a little breakdown during her final year of premed. It happens, you know. These high-achieving kids go off to college and overextend themselves on all fronts. The next thing you know, they're breaking down or turning to drugs. I'm just thankful Isla didn't end up involved with the drugs."

"I understand." He gave Mrs. Morris a knowing nod. "We'll find her, see that she's safe."

"I would appreciate it so much," Mrs. Morris said, gratitude in her eyes and her smile. "Remember," she said to Leah, "the spare key is under the fairy."

Mrs. Morris reminded Leah of the address for the Fox Lake home. She went on and on about the amenities and the lovely views. Leah nodded and made agreeable sounds, when it was obvious she had no idea where this retreat was located, much less what it offered.

But they were about to find out.

Leah hugged Isla's mother and promised to keep her apprised. Mrs. Morris promised the same. By the time Owen and Leah were back in the car, she was shaking.

"I have no idea about this lake house." She turned to Owen. "I have never been there with Isla. She has never mentioned that her mother had one. It's true I'm not big on swimming in anything other than pools where I can see the bottom, but I have never been to that lake house. And Isla never told me about any sort of breakdown."

And there it was, the first crack in the beloved, seemingly steadfast friendship. One of the two had not been sharing *everything*.

"Maybe Isla was taking a friend with whom she had a physical relationship to the lake house," Owen suggested. "She may have told her mother it was you to avoid questions." He wasn't buying that story just yet, but if it made Leah feel better in the short term, that was the immediate objective. He started the car and pulled away from the curb.

"That's possible," Leah agreed after pondering the suggestion. "Her mother was always after her about the future and starting a family. She didn't want Isla to wait until it was too late. You know the routine. 'Get married and make me some grandbabies.'" Leah laughed but the sound held no humor; it was more sad than anything. "Isla does not want children. She's all about her career. I'm not sure how she'll ever break it to her mother."

For Leah's sake, he hoped that was her friend's only dreaded secret. Though Owen now suspected it was just the tip of the iceberg.

Chapter Five

Morris Lake House
Fox Lake, 12:50 p.m.

Owen brought the car to a stop in the small area of gravel just off the narrow road provided for parking at the rear of the house. Leah was awed by the view, for sure. The house was perched so close to the shore that it looked as if it might slide off into the water at any second. It was breathtakingly beautiful. Very private, with a wooded area separating it from the nearest neighbor.

Aside from the one Owen had just parked, there was no vehicle there. If Isla was here, someone had dropped her off or she had walked. Leah was confident that was not the case. This place was nearly an hour's drive from the city.

As they climbed out of the vehicle, Leah couldn't ignore the very bad feeling mounting inside her. Something about this situation was very, very wrong.

"I have never been here," she said to the man standing next to her. "I can't imagine why Isla told her mother I came here with her—unless it's...it's like you said and she was covering for who she was really bringing." She shook her head. "But that's so un-Isla-like. She always seems in charge and straightforward." Leah moved her head side to side in dismay. "She's the most independent and put-together person I've ever known. I just can't see her sneaking around. I don't even see a reason for her to have told her mother about coming here, much less making up who came with her."

"I'll look for that key," he said, rather than comment on her assessment.

She got it. He didn't know Isla. What could he say?

While he located the fairy statue and the key hidden beneath it, she took in more of that amazing view. After a moment, she started helping with his search. It took a minute. The shrubs next to the less-than-two-feet-tall statue had grown so that it was very nearly concealed. A good thing, Leah supposed, to prevent anyone from noticing it and looking under it.

On the stoop, Owen knocked several times, but there was no answer. Finally, he inserted the key and unlocked the door. Leah held her breath as they dared to cross the threshold. Inside was bright, even though the lights were off. The abundance of windows across the lake side of the house ensured good lighting. The air was stuffy and a little too warm. The air-conditioning was either off or set high enough that it hadn't kicked on. Leah's nose wrinkled. There was an underlying unpleasant odor. Maybe from being closed up for a while.

As with many homes on the water, the front of the house faced the lake. With that in mind, the entrance door, which was actually at the back of the house next to the small parking area, led into a little mudroom and then the kitchen. The kitchen was the usual cottage-style and wide open to the rest of the central part of the one-story house. Without the interruption of walls, it flowed straight into the living area, where several conversation groupings were scattered around those large front windows. One grouping included a television while the rest came with only the view—which was more than sufficiently inspiring. A bookcase stuffed with books and comfortable seating made the space even more inviting.

"Isla?" It seemed obvious enough that she wasn't in the house, but Leah felt compelled to call out her name.

The house was strangely quiet. And so still—eerily so, like the water beyond all those windows.

Leah turned to the professional in matters such as this one. "Should we search the rest of the house?" She wasn't sure of the protocol in these situations. Her instinct was to tear through the house calling her friend's name.

"We're here," he said. "The owner gave us permission to be here. We might as well see if there are any indications Isla or anyone else has been in the house at some point during the last three or four days."

A perfectly logical analysis. "I'll take the bedrooms."

Leah turned down a short hall to the left. There were four doors: two on her right—the lake side—one at the end and one on the left. The door on the left was a bathroom. Neat and airy, very beachy looking. Typical vintage tile and fixtures. A surprisingly large shower for a house of this age. The inside of the toilet bowl had a dark line of old mold or mineral deposits circling it, suggesting it hadn't been flushed in a while.

The two doors across the hall led to smallish bedrooms furnished with double beds and a single dresser each. The focal point in both rooms was the window looking out over the lake. No indications that anyone had been in either of the two rooms in the past few weeks. Nothing unexpected in the tiny closets. Each of the dressers sported a fine layer of undisturbed dust.

The more Leah looked, the more worried she grew. *Where are you, Isla?*

The door at the end of the short hall would likely lead to the larger bedroom. So far, the trip all this way had been a waste of time. But at least it got her out of the city and away from the horrors of the past few days.

Leah drew her hand back when she would have opened the final door. On some level, she suddenly wished she had worn gloves. She had never been to this house, no matter what Isla had told her mother. Today was her first time here. Now her prints would be all over the place as if Isla had been telling the truth.

She closed her eyes and shook her head. This whole thing was making her paranoid.

Whatever Isla's reason for telling her mother that story, it was not related to the missing Raymond Douglas or anything else untoward.

With renewed determination, Leah grasped the knob and gave it a twist. The door opened. Instantly, an overwhelming, sickening metallic odor hit her in the face. The space was nearly pitch black. A frown tugged at her lips. Why so dark?

She felt along the wall next to the doorframe and flipped the switch. Then her hand went over her nose and mouth to ward off the stench. Directly in front of her was the bed, larger than the others. But unlike the others, the covers were tousled. There were handcuffs on the headboard and footboard. Also unlike the others, the windows were covered, blocking that fabulous view of the lake.

"What the…?" She stepped fully into the room, surveyed more closely the windows that extended half the width of the room and then stretched around the corner and ran down half the length of the other side of the room as well. The interior shutters were all closed.

She shivered. But it was the smell that unsettled her the most. What was that unbearable odor?

A step, then another took her beyond the bed that stood in the center of the room. On the other side was a large circle of something rusty and thick-looking.

Blood.

Leah's first thought was to scream, but the sound wouldn't emerge from her throat.

She backed out of the room and turned, bumping square into Owen.

"Nothing anywhere in the main living area or in the laundry room," he told her. "That smell—" He took in her expression, then frowned. "What's wrong?"

"The bedroom," she said, her voice scarcely a whisper. Then she hitched her thumb toward the room behind her. "There's blood. A lot of blood."

"Stay here." He ushered her aside and disappeared through the door Leah had left standing open.

She pressed her hands to her face and struggled to hold back tears. That couldn't be Isla's blood. No. Her friend could not be hurt…or dead. Images of Raymond being dragged across that kitchen floor…blood trickling down the side of his head…flashed erratically in her head.

What if the blood belonged to Raymond? What if he had been brought here from the restaurant? But why here? Did he and Isla know each other that well? Why hadn't she told Leah? It made no sense.

Was he the one who would come here with Isla? That would explain the visits she'd claimed to her mother were with Leah.

But why? It just didn't feel reasonable.

If Isla were involved with Raymond, why on earth would she try to set Leah up with him? The idea was ridiculous.

Stop, just stop. Whatever had happened...it wasn't good.

Had someone been held against their will and then died here? Or were the handcuffs part of a sex game? The blood might have been from a situation that got out of control... Was that why Isla was not returning calls? Was she in hiding? Injured?

Oh God.

Just calm down.

There was no body. There was only blood. This didn't mean anyone was dead.

The sound of Owen's voice snapped her out of the troubling thoughts. She heard him say the detective's name. He was calling the police.

This was bad.

She steadied herself. Of course he was calling the police. Someone had been gravely injured in this house. Someone...not Isla. *Please not Isla.*

Even if it was an accident, something had happened here. The police had to be called.

When Owen finished his call, he came out into the hall. "Detective Lambert is sending a forensic team to investigate. We're to wait outside until he arrives. If the team gets here first, they will come inside and start processing the scene."

The scene. This was a crime scene.

Just like the restaurant had been a crime scene, only no one had believed her. Like her and Isla's apartment. Dear God, what was happening?

She cleared her throat, braced herself for the answer to the question she was about to ask. "Is that enough blood to suggest whoever lost it died from his or her injury?"

"It's a lot of blood, Leah." He spoke softly, kindly, as if he knew the answer already and wanted to keep her calm. "Let's just wait to see what the forensic team has to say before we jump to any conclusions."

Her stomach lurched. "I need to...to go outside."

She hurried through the house until she was out the back door. Her stomach churned with the need to evacuate its contents. *Deep breath.* Two, three more deep breaths later, and the nausea settled down.

For a while she paced. There were so many things she wanted to ask, but who would have the answers? Not her top-notch private investigator, not Isla's mother and certainly not Detective Lambert. How could they? No one was here. Neither Isla nor Raymond were at the places they lived or worked. Isla's mother had not heard from her.

This was...unbelievable. Beyond bizarre.

Owen sat down on the bench that stood next to the back door. Above his head was a sign that said *Welcome. To what?* Leah mused. *Hell?* She collapsed next to him.

"Isla would have called already if she was okay." Her gaze collided with his. "She's not, and I'm terrified that the blood in there confirms it."

"I want you to think carefully, Leah," Owen said with infinite calmness and a sense of reassurance she wanted desperately to latch on to. "When was the last time you were in contact with Isla?"

Leah closed her eyes and ordered her mind to stop twisting with scary thoughts. "We were both home most of the day Saturday. We were just relaxing and reading. Later that evening—about seven, I think—she left for work. I dressed for the date that will go down in infamy as the world's absolute worst blind date."

He smiled sadly. "You haven't heard from her since around seven on Saturday evening."

Leah nodded. Three days, basically. There was no denying it now. Even without the blood, Isla would never be out of contact for that length of time. Especially with her mother. Isla often said that she was all her mother had since her brother never seemed to have time for either of them.

She and Isla were both the single support systems for their mothers. Not that Isla's mother wasn't able to take care of herself like Leah's mother, but when she needed something, Isla was her go-to person. Just as Leah had been for her mother since her father died.

That familiar old pain arced through her, amplified by the dread knotting in her gut. Who would want to hurt Isla?

Why? She was such a good person.

"When Detective Lambert arrives," Owen said, interrupting her troubling thoughts, "he'll have a lot of questions. I want you to take your time and think carefully before you answer. If during his questioning I interrupt whatever you're about to say, stop immediately and say nothing more. All right?"

She nodded but didn't really comprehend why it was

necessary to be so careful. "I don't understand. Is there some reason I should be worried about what he might think of what I say?"

Of course there was. Leah didn't want to believe it, but this was bad, and somehow she was connected to it.

"Sometimes our words can be misconstrued or taken out of context—especially when we're emotional," Owen explained. "It's obvious to me that someone is setting you up. We just need to proceed with caution until Lambert understands that as well."

The bottom dropped out of her stomach right after the words *someone is setting you up*. Who would do that? She had friends. But only one close friend, and that was Isla. There was no way Isla would be setting her up. Besides, Leah had no real money or other marketable assets that anyone might want. She had a job, but she barely made enough to keep her head above water. She owned nothing except a few odd pieces of furniture, and she had no social life. She'd just appropriated the better part of her savings to figure out this insane mess.

"Why?" She searched his eyes in hopes of finding the answer there. "Why would anyone pick me for this, whatever it is?"

"Two reasons, as far as I can see," he said. "You have a record—however distant—of being involved with unsavory types."

Leah groaned. "I'm a model human for most of my life, and no one notices. I screw up once and get involved with a thug, and I'm a suspected criminal forevermore."

Owen shrugged. "Look at it like getting hacked on social media. It's the people who would never dream of or even know how to hack an account who get hacked. It's the same people who want to believe the best in everyone they meet. Those who trust maybe more than they should. Sometimes we just don't see what's right in front of us."

"You believe this comes down to Isla." He didn't have to say it outright. She got it. At this point, even she was admittedly having difficulty denying the possibility. But why would her friend do all this? What did she have to gain?

"It's the most logical possibility, given what we know at this time," he confirmed. "But remember, we're going on only a small amount of knowledge. There is still a lot we haven't figured out. Many things can happen in seventy-two hours. We are only aware of a few of those events. This entire situation could change direction at any moment."

He didn't say change for the worse, but she understood that was what he meant.

This could get exponentially worse.

JUST OVER AN hour later, a dark sedan arrived at the lake house. Not the black car that had been following her; Leah hadn't seen it since arriving at the safe house. Owen had made sure the driver was unable to follow. The man had evasive driving tactics down to a science.

While she watched, Detective Lambert emerged from the sedan. Before he'd closed the door, a white van sporting the Chicago PD logo arrived, and an official police cruiser as well. Leah wondered if this location was still in Lambert's jurisdiction. Maybe it didn't matter, since the situation was related to his ongoing case. Or so it would seem.

"Ms. Gerard," he said as he approached her, "this isn't an address I had associated with you."

"This lake house belongs to Isla's family."

"You've been here before," Lambert suggested. A reasonable assumption.

Before Leah could answer, Owen explained, "We visited Mrs. Morris this morning to see if she has heard from her daughter. She has not. She suggested we look here. She gave us the location of the house and the key to go inside. As soon as we discovered the blood, we called you and came outside."

"Had you been here before?" Lambert asked Leah again.

"No." She shook her head. "Mrs. Morris seems to think I have. She said Isla told her on several occasions that she was coming to the lake house with me, but that isn't true. I've never been here before today."

"We suspect," Owen said, "that Isla was giving her mother Leah's name to conceal the identity of the person she was actually bringing here."

"Any motive you're aware of that would prompt her to take such a step?"

"We have found no motive as of yet," Owen admitted.

"How long will it take," Leah asked, "to figure out whose blood that is?" Her heart squeezed. Someone would have to talk to Mrs. Morris. She needed to be aware of what was happening. What a nightmare this would be for her until she knew what had actually happened.

"It's difficult to say," Lambert conceded. "We'll need to find out her blood type, as well as that of Raymond Douglas, and then we'll do DNA testing using Isla's mother and, I suppose, one of Douglas's children, assuming all involved will cooperate. If not, we have other ways. Hair from a brush or comb they used. A toothbrush."

The worry would eat Leah alive before then. "Can your forensic people determine how long the blood has been in that room?"

She had seen both Isla and Raymond on Saturday evening.

"That, we can do, and fairly quickly." Lambert hitched his head toward the house. "I should get inside and see what we have." He hesitated. "If you would wait here, I'm sure I will have more questions."

Oh yeah. Leah was confident he would have plenty more questions. Questions she could not answer.

As she and Owen sat in the quiet of the outdoors for a few moments, she thought about what she had seen in that room besides the blood. Handcuffs. Someone had presumably kept Isla or Raymond against their will. Or it was a part of some sex game gone wrong.

Either possibility made her feel sick. Worse, it was possible he or she had been tortured—she thought of the blood—and killed.

Leah wished there was a way to protect Isla's mother from all this until they knew more. She would be devastated. And then, if the blood turned out to be Raymond's...

Then what? Isla was still missing. Something had happened to her, whether it was in this house or elsewhere. She was missing. The police needed to be looking for her. Yet somehow, this all felt as if it were moving in slow motion. Yes, the detective was here, but nothing seemed to be getting done. No answers appeared to have been found.

The weight of it all settled on Leah's shoulders, and

she desperately wished she could shake it off. But that was impossible.

Owen leaned forward, braced his forearms on his knees and turned his face to hers. "Isla set you up on a blind date with Raymond Douglas. When Douglas disappeared, Isla disappeared. If one of the two set this up, Leah—and I can't see any way around that possibility—they set you up to take the fall for whatever the finale is to be. But the real questions are, which one and for what reason?"

"I can give you a reason—five million of them, as a matter of fact."

Leah and Owen turned to the detective who had just walked out the back door.

"What?" Leah demanded.

Owen put his hand on her arm and said to the detective, "We're listening."

"The ex-wife, Louise, is the one who first told me about the insurance policy. When I spoke with the insurance company, I learned there was not one but two beneficiaries—who would receive five million each."

Leah remembered him saying there was an insurance policy, but he'd only mentioned the ex-wife.

"The sole beneficiary was Louise until just a few months ago. Douglas changed his policy at that time. Half of the proceeds go to his ex-wife, and the other half goes to you, Leah."

"What?" She shook her head. "No." That was absurd. She shook her head again. "Why would he leave me anything? We hardly know each other. We'd never even met before two weeks ago."

"That, Ms. Gerard, is the five-million-dollar question," Lambert said.

No, no, no. This simply could not be right. It was completely ridiculous. Outrageous.

This situation grew more inexplicable by the day. It was as if, once the momentum started, there was no stopping it. The absurdities just kept piling up.

Leah turned to Owen. "I do not know Raymond Douglas. Not like that. There is no way he would want to leave me anything. This is all wrong."

But how would she make anyone believe her?

Chapter Six

4:50 p.m.

Owen spotted the black sedan in his rearview mirror less than a minute after they drove away from the lake house. He glanced at his passenger. She stared out her window, arms crossed protectively over her chest.

This day had been particularly tough for her. She had every reason to fear that her friend was gravely injured or perhaps dead. The situation with the missing date, Raymond Douglas, had grown exponentially more complicated with the insurance-beneficiary revelation. At this point, all Leah had was her word that she did not know Douglas other than as a potential blind date. Isla was not here to confirm, and the other friend, Maya Ortiz, who had been with Leah and Isla the night Leah briefly met Douglas, was no help.

According to Lambert, Ortiz had no idea if Leah and Douglas had dated once or a dozen times since that accidental encounter. She claimed to have been preoccupied that night with watching an ex-boyfriend she had spotted in the crowd at the club. If there were other newly discovered details, Lambert wasn't sharing. Owen was surprised the detective had revealed as much as he had.

As if all the questions and the troubling lack of any ability to confirm her statements wasn't bad enough, Leah was faced with yet another blow: Lambert asked for permission to search the apartment she and Isla shared. Owen had recommended she agree to the search. With the discovery at the lake house, obtaining a search warrant for the apartment was a mere formality—no judge would deny the request. Leah's cooperation was necessary to prevent any additional suspicion being cast her way. She had nothing to hide, and Lambert needed to see that.

The problem was, her innocence didn't mean someone hadn't planted something to make her look guilty, which was why the two of them were going straight to the apartment right now to look around. Bolling, the building manager, had confirmed that the police had released the apartment and the repairs had been started. Owen and Leah could go into the apartment, but there was still work to be done before she could move back in. Bolling would provide them access.

Owen checked the rearview mirror once more. The sedan was still behind them.

He might as well wait until they were in the city to bother with losing him. If he could somehow manage to get the license plate number, that might prove useful in identifying the driver.

"He's following us again," Leah said, sitting up straighter. She'd obviously spotted the tail in her side mirror.

"He is," Owen confirmed. "Unless he makes an aggressive move, we'll just pretend we don't notice until we're in the city. Losing him will be simpler, and arriving at our destination before he finds us again will be far more likely."

"Okay." She relaxed into her seat, but her attention remained on the mirror.

Rather than allow her to fixate on that troubling detail, Owen opted for making conversation. "Tell me about when you met Isla."

Leah glanced at him. Her brown eyes reflected the increasing worry haunting her. She had beautiful eyes—deep brown, and such a generous oval shape. She was a very attractive woman. Her quiet nature made him curious, knowing her history as he did. Those painful years after the Chris Painter situation had changed her, it seemed. He wondered if she would ever allow her adventurous spirit to slip past all those tight restraints put into place in an attempt at self-preservation. It was a shame that a single incident stole so much of what made her who she was. Maturity and wisdom were always valuable, but one's true spirit should always have a place inside the normal course of development.

"She had just finished her first year of medical school, and I was deep into my undergrad work." She stared forward. "I felt so far behind before I even started. Most people start college right after high school. Here I was, more than four years later." She sighed. "Once I arrived in Chicago, the first order of business was to find a place to live, and truthfully, I was drowning in uncertainty. The only good thing was that my student loan had come through, so I was okay with the education costs. I had decided I might just survive. The first couple of years, I managed by the skin of my teeth and the bit of extra allowance in my student loans. Eventually, I landed the position at the library, and I was in heaven. Isla and one of her friends were there one night for a workshop, and that was the beginning."

"You said Isla was already in the apartment you share now."

"Yes, she'd been there awhile. Later, I learned she hadn't really needed a roommate, but she wanted to help me and decided to make the offer." She fell silent a moment. "Not long after I moved in, Maya—Isla's friend, and mine, too, eventually—made some remark about Isla always taking on projects. I was offended at first, but in time we worked it out."

"This Maya," he glanced at Leah, "never apologized or elaborated?"

"No." She laughed dryly. "Maya does not apologize for anything. She has a rich daddy and an even richer new boyfriend. She has her master's in journalism. She works for one of the major networks now. She is utterly unrepentant. But she is Isla's friend, so I have to like her."

"You and Isla became friends quickly." From all Leah had said so far, their relationship evolved swiftly and deeply.

"Over the fall," Leah explained. "By Christmas, I was moving in, and we were like sisters."

"What about Isla's dating habits? Does she date frequently? Different people, or was there anyone who lasted longer than the others? Maybe someone who left her upset?"

"Unlike me," Leah said, "Isla is very social. That said, she's as happy with a group of girlfriends as she is with a guy. In the time I've known her, she has not dated anyone seriously or for any length of time. There were a few who got past the third date but none who lasted more than a month or so. She is thoroughly focused on the future. I mean, totally dedicated to a singular goal. She has this plan and is determined that nothing will stop her or get in the way. I've tried really hard to do the same. She's helped me a lot with moving forward and not looking back."

"The man, Chris Painter ..." Owen braked for a traffic light and spent a moment studying her. "Were you in love with him?"

Though she had been young, her heart could still be broken. Sometimes an old wound like that one was difficult to heal.

She leaned against the headrest. "I was as in love with him as a naive eighteen-year-old, incredibly overprotected girl could be. I was devastated when he just vanished. I searched for him. Confronted his friends and a few of his enemies. Had the bejesus scared out of me more than once and ended up in the ER with a black eye, busted lip and fractured rib." She met his gaze. "There are some bears one shouldn't poke."

He could see the fearless girl-woman storming into the presence of dangerous thugs and demanding answers. She was lucky she hadn't gotten herself killed.

"At that point I stopped trying to force the truth out of the people he'd surrounded himself with. I went home with my tail between my legs and told myself falling for a guy like Chris would never happen again. And it hasn't. But it took time and distance to put it behind me. I changed myself and my life over and over until I realized that it wasn't my physical being that needed to change—

it was my mental self. My attitude and personal boundaries. I'm still a work in progress."

"I think you're doing great." He checked the rearview mirror once more. Their tail kept his distance but remained vigilant.

"Well…" She drew in a big breath and released it slowly. "If I don't end up charged with murder, maybe I'll be able to keep moving forward." She fell silent for a time. "But I have to tell you, Owen, I'm worried. The trouble just keeps stacking up, and every time something new is discovered, it points to me."

"That is the way a good setup works," he told her with a sidelong look to punctuate it. "Which is why I believe whatever we're wading into was well planned, perhaps for a considerable period of time."

"But how do I prove my innocence when I have no *proof*? No one besides Isla and Raymond know when I first met him. No one but those two know Saturday night was our first and only date—not that it was an actual date. And until Mrs. Morris told me that Isla claimed I went to the lake house with her occasionally, I was certain she was as much a victim as me—maybe more so since she's missing. But now I don't know. Nothing we learn makes sense. Nothing Lambert throws our way makes sense—like that insurance policy."

"We will find the right answers," he promised. "I'm very good at my work, Leah. You can count on that."

She turned toward him fully, her expression steeped in concern. "I am counting on that. I mean, *really* counting on it."

Gerard/Morris Apartment
Chestnut Street, 5:15 p.m.

"KEEP YOUR ATTENTION FORWARD," Owen said when he shut off the engine. "Don't look at him. Just ignore him completely. We'll go inside and have a look around. Then when we head for the safe house, we'll lose him."

Leah nodded. When they'd reached Chicago proper, Owen decided to let the guy in the sedan follow them to the apartment. It wasn't like he didn't already know where it was. Brilliantly, Owen had called a fellow Colby investigator and asked him to do a drive-by and snag the guy's license plate number. Leah was impressed with the idea. The sooner they found out who the guy was, the better. She assumed he was a hired spy or maybe even an assassin working for the bad guys. The problem was, who were the bad guys? And why was Leah their target? Or at least one of their targets, it seemed.

Was the bad guy the person who'd dragged Raymond out of the kitchen, dead or unconscious? Or the best friend she had come to think of as a sister?

The mere thought had more of those knots twisting in Leah's belly.

She and Owen opened their doors and exited the car. Leah fixated on the sweltering heat and the drooping flowers in the pots on the steps that led to the entrance of her building. This really had been a very hot summer. Sadly, it just wasn't getting any better. All sorts of little fires were cropping up around her as her life fell apart one piece at a time.

She entered the code and Owen opened the main entrance door. They walked together to the stairs and climbed up to the second floor. Thinking back on their conversation in the car, she was surprised at how easy talking to him was. Usually, she had a difficult time discussing personal relationships or details with others—especially strangers. And he was a stranger. No matter that he was so comfortable to be around…to talk to. Honestly, he didn't feel like a stranger at all. He somehow made sharing comfortable. Then again, she supposed it was part of his job to know how to mine cooperation from a subject. But the way their conversations developed, they never felt anything but completely natural and well-intentioned.

Bolling waited outside the apartment. The repair work was moving along. A door had been framed in, but the drywall around it had not been finished, and there was still the painting and necessary trim work. She was actually surprised it had happened so quickly.

The manager unlocked the door and passed the key to Leah. "This is the key you'll need when the repairs are completed. Shouldn't take more than another day."

That really was fast. "Thank you."

Bolling nodded and headed back downstairs.

Walking into her apartment now, knowing all that she knew, felt strange. It no longer felt like home. And certainly no longer felt safe.

Where was Isla? Had she been injured? What in the world had happened to Raymond, and what did any of it have to do with Leah?

The most damning and startling piece of this puzzle was the fact that she had been named a beneficiary on his life insurance policy. The idea was ludicrous, irrational. Totally out of left field.

How could she be a beneficiary of his when she hardly knew the man?

"Let's start in this main room," Owen suggested. "We touch everything. No matter how small or seemingly insignificant. Whatever is here, we want to see it and feel it, as well as recognize its reason for being in this space. A piece of the puzzle could be hiding in plain sight... anywhere in this apartment."

He was right. *Deep breath.* "Okay."

They started at the door. Checked every piece of furniture. Inside and under the drawers. Behind doors on the lower portion of the one large bookcase and inside every single book that lined its open shelves. Every item discovered was picked up and examined. Leah found a couple of appointment cards she'd forgotten about entirely. One was from the dentist's office for her annual cleaning. The other was for a meeting with her mother's doctor.

When they had handled every item in the main living area, they moved on to the bedrooms. There were only two, and each had its own bath.

"I'll take your room," Owen said. "You take Isla's. It's important to determine if anything looks out of place. I wouldn't know, because I've never met Isla or been in her room. As for your room, I'm sure you would have noticed anything out of place already. I'll just be a fresh second look."

Made sense, even though Leah was embarrassed at the idea of him going through her things. "Sounds good." He was right about her needing to be the one who went through Isla's things.

In Isla's private space, Leah first got down onto all fours and looked under the bed, the night table and the dresser. All stood on legs that left about fifteen inches of space beneath them. Prime territory for storage, particularly under the bed. Nothing but a few dust bunnies. Isla wasn't one to hoard, even a little bit. Then Leah moved on to the window. She checked the drapes and the chair and the table that sat in front of it. Isla's desk was on that same wall. Leah surveyed the cluttered desktop and awakened her friend's computer in hopes of perusing her email and having a quick look at her search history.

The computer required a password.

Leah wasn't even going to attempt figuring it out. Instead, she surveyed the notepad and two sticky notes posted on the sleek wood surface. One was a list of personal items she needed. The other sticky note reminded Isla to talk to her boss about a raise.

"You go, Isla," Leah murmured.

Leah moved on, checking the drawers in Isla's dresser. Nothing unexpected or seemingly out of place so far.

Next, she checked the closet. Lots and lots of clothes. Isla really was a clotheshorse, but she shopped smartly, never paying full price for anything, she often bragged.

Even after a thorough second look of the room, Leah found nothing that didn't belong.

She walked out of the room just as Owen exited hers.

"Anything?" she asked. "I found nothing in Isla's room."

"Is this yours?" He opened his hand, revealing a black cell phone. Smaller than the one she carried.

"No." She pulled her phone from her pants pockets. "This is my phone."

"This one," he said, "was tucked into your lingerie drawer."

The idea that he had touched her *lingerie*, as he'd put it, made her heart thump hard against her sternum. She hadn't even considered he would have to filter through her most intimate apparel. Ridiculous. Of course, searching each drawer was necessary.

She shook her head, not daring to touch the phone. If she didn't touch it, her prints wouldn't be on it. "I've never seen it before."

"The battery is dead. We should charge it up and see what we find."

"I agree." She folded her arms over her chest and suppressed a shiver. The idea of what else they might find was terrifying.

Owen had been so smart and definitely one step ahead to suggest they come here and have a look. If not, Lambert would have found that phone and assumed it was hers. How had it gotten into her room? Given all that had happened, she could just imagine what kind of incriminating "evidence" was on it.

Owen slid the phone into his back pocket. "If you need to get anything else while we're here, you should pack it up—and have a look around just in case. Then we'll get going."

She nodded and went into her room. Leah tried to center on what she might need and not think about what he'd found, but it wasn't easy. She grabbed a dressier shirt in case she needed something more than the T-shirts she had taken to the safe house. Then she remembered she had forgotten lotion, so she picked that up too. And a nightshirt; she'd completely forgotten to take anything for sleeping. With a final quick look around to ensure nothing was missing or there that shouldn't be, she decided she was done. Her overnight bag was already at the safe house, so she opted to just carry the three items.

She went to the living room, where Owen waited.

"Got everything you need?"

"I think so."

He grinned. "Now to ghost our nosy friend."

That made her smile. The guy in the black car wouldn't be happy, she imagined.

But when Owen opened the door for her, her smile died.

Detective Lambert and his forensic team were standing in the corridor.

"What a surprise," the detective said. "Did you find whatever you were looking for?"

Leah held her breath...didn't dare speak.

"Just dropped by for a few items she needed," Owen said with a gesture toward the items she clutched.

Good grief. She'd completely forgotten she was holding anything. The craziness was getting to her, making her paranoid.

"I needed a few more things," she said, her voice a little high, a little shaky.

Lambert nodded. "Well, if you're quite finished, we'll get started on our search."

"Of course." Leah slipped past him, her heart pounding way too fast.

What if he spotted the bulge of that cell phone in Owen's pocket? What if he decided it was necessary to pat them down like the police often did to suspects in the movies? The phone would only make her look guiltier.

Worry twisted like razors inside her.

Owen joined her in the corridor, and they walked casually toward the stairwell. He set the pace. Slow and steady. She forced her respiration to slow and followed his example. No one hurried after them, demanding to check their pockets. But she didn't relax until they were out of the building and in his car.

Once they were driving away, he said, "I have to make a quick stop before I lose this guy."

She frowned. "Where?"

"Anywhere." He shot her a grin. "Just long enough to make sure our shadow didn't put a tracking device on the car."

She hadn't even considered the person watching her—following them—might do something so obviously smart in a situation like this. Good thing she had this man on her side.

Her gaze lingered on Owen's profile. *A really good thing.*

Chapter Seven

Colby Agency Safe House
East Elm Street, 7:20 p.m.

There had been no tracking device on the car.

Losing their tail had been fairly easy, or maybe he just hadn't tried so hard to keep up with them. Either way, Leah had watched Owen expertly outmaneuver him. They made it back to the safe house without the trouble following them.

Now, seated on a stool at the kitchen island, Leah watched as Owen plugged up the phone he had found in her underwear drawer. Heat climbed up her throat and rested on her cheeks each time she thought of him touching her underthings. Thankfully, she had packed most of her favorites when preparing to come here, leaving the less-worn pairs in the drawer. Who wanted such a handsome guy—any guy, really—discovering she preferred comfortable panties?

She shook herself mentally. What was she thinking? Someone had, in some way, disappeared at least two people she knew, and that same person seemed to want to pin the blame on her. This was not the time to be wondering what this man thought of her underwear.

"Here we go."

The screen of the phone lit up.

Leah held her breath. Maybe now they would find some answers or at least a clue of some sort as to what the heck was going on. Her pulse gained an extra beat every second or so as she watched him scroll, pausing now and then perhaps to read. The furrowing of his brow and the stony set of his jaw made her stomach sink.

Finally, he stopped and looked up at her. "I need you to scan the call list and see if you recognize any of the numbers. Then go to the text messages and read those to see if any of it is familiar to you or if you recognize the way the messages are worded. We all have our favorite buzzwords and sentence structures."

Cold leeched from her limbs. "Okay." She held out her hand, and he placed the seemingly harmless device on her palm.

Leah swallowed around the lump swelling in her throat and concentrated on the small screen. The one currently displayed was the log of recent calls. There were no names, just phone numbers and the word *Him*. The call log ended on Saturday night and only went back five days. From late on Monday of last week until this past Saturday—the night Raymond disappeared. Isla, too, apparently.

There were nine calls, one each day until Saturday, and then there were four. All to or from the same number.

Raymond's.

Fear trickled through her chest. Ordinarily, she wouldn't have remembered a phone number so easily, except his last four digits were 1001. It had to be his. But just in case she was wrong, she reached for her cell phone and checked the call log for the one time she had spoken to him. There it was: 312-555-1001.

"The person using this phone was talking to Raymond." She looked up at Owen. "It wasn't me. I swear."

He nodded once. "Read the text messages."

The urge to throw the phone across the room and run was nearly overwhelming. She did not want to read those messages. It didn't matter that they had absolutely not come from her or been sent to her. This was not right.

Deep breath. She forced her fingers to work, tapping and swiping as needed until the Messages app opened. There was only one listing. She tapped on *Him*. The next screen opened to a long thread of message exchanges.

Are you ready for our big night???

That one was from whoever *Him* was.

Can't wait. Are you sure you're ready?

This message was sent via the phone found in her underwear drawer...the one she held in her hand at this very moment.

Leah forced herself to keep reading, though the rock in her gut seemed to be trying to push upward into her throat.

Him: Oh yeah. We have everything we need.

Underwear-Drawer Phone User: How can I wait as long as this might take?

Him: Patience. The five mil will be ours.

The ability to breathe grew harder and harder.

Underwear-Drawer Phone User: Sand, sun and water... forever.

Him: Just the two of us...

There were several more but nothing relevant, just the mushy back-and-forth of two lovers planning some sort of getaway.

She stared up at the man standing on the other side of the island. His blue eyes watched her intently. He would be analyzing her reaction...her every word. Deciding if he should continue trusting her.

Leah swallowed. "I didn't send these messages. I have never seen this phone before. This is not me." She shook her head, the movement stilted. "Someone else did this."

Owen took the phone from her and set it aside. "Is there anyone else who might have a key to your apartment? Besides you and Isla?"

Leah struggled to steady her respiration. She needed to think rationally, which was difficult with her heart racing and her thoughts in a tailspin. Who would do this? "No one that I'm aware of. Isla said I was her first roommate."

"But she could have given a key to a boyfriend or long-term lover," he suggested.

"I guess so, but she never mentioned having given a key to anyone." Then again, why would she? Leah felt sick at where this was pointing. "I didn't know Raymond Douglas before two weeks ago, and I had no idea he planned to ask me on a date until one week ago." She searched Owen's eyes. "How am I ever going to prove I'm telling the truth?" She stared at the phone lying on the counter. "Everything keeps coming back to me."

"This phone—" he gestured to the one he'd found in her drawer "—is commonly called a burner phone. I'm sure you've heard the term."

She nodded. "On television, but I've never known anyone who used one in real life." She frowned. "That might not be true. Chris..." She took a moment to ride out the uneasiness she always felt at saying his name out loud. "He and his thug buddies may have used them. I can't be sure, but it would make sense."

"That's a good guess," Owen agreed. "Whoever bought this one wanted to make it seem as if you were communicating with Raymond in a way that couldn't be traced. And it couldn't...not to you, except for the fact that the phone was hidden in your bedroom to do exactly that. Lead those investigating the case to you."

It couldn't be Isla. It just couldn't be.

"In my opinion," he went on, "the most telling aspect of what we have here is the fact that Raymond didn't use one. This suggests that whoever masterminded this plot wanted it known that the user of this burner phone—you, presumably—was interacting with Raymond. That step was deliberate."

Fighting a new bout of vertigo, Leah considered this for a moment. Owen was right. If the whole thing that went down on Saturday night was supposed to be some secret setup, all parties involved would have remained anonymous by using burner phones...*except* the one whom they wanted to get caught.

Bile stirred in her belly.

She struggled to articulate the fear pressing against her

chest. "Are you suggesting that the person pretending to be me was actually setting Raymond up to be murdered, or are you saying they both wanted the police to believe he was being set up to be murdered?"

Owen's brow lined in thought. "This is where the situation could go either way. We have no definitive proof one way or the other."

"What about the life insurance policy?" Leah asked.

"Obviously, that detail would make it appear as though you were plotting to kill him, since you stood to gain five mil. This phone suggests the same. Except, if that is the goal, the rest of the plan seems counterintuitive."

"How so?" Leah's head was spinning. None of this made sense to her. It only proved to her that someone had set her up to take the fall for murder.

"If the goal was to get the five million," he explained, "you need a body or the patience to wait a very long time until there is irrefutable proof that the missing person is in fact dead—at least, for all intents and purposes. Why set up a scam like this if the payoff is going to be that far down the road? Or denied. There has to be an official determination that Raymond Douglas is dead before there is an insurance payoff to anyone."

"Are you saying the insurance policy is a ruse? Just something else to throw the police off…what?"

"We can't be sure at this point. But personally…" He gave her a critical look. "If I were Raymond Douglas, I would be worried. With what we have right now, I see no way anyone stands to win at this game without a body—*his* body."

Leah didn't want to believe what she was about to say, but at this juncture, what else could she believe? "The most likely scenario—for now, anyway—is that Isla and Raymond planned all this. She had access to my room, to my schedule...to my whole life." It hurt to say the words out loud. "And she knew Raymond. She downplayed her knowledge of him for my benefit. As much as I don't want to believe that's possible, I can't see any other scenario where this comes together logically."

"It's a difficult reality to accept," he agreed. "But, as you say, at this time it's the most logical theory."

"How could Isla and I have been friends all this time—shared all that we have shared—and none of it matter when she came up with this plan?" Leah wondered if Isla had ever really cared about her. Had her taking on a roommate been a setup from the beginning? Surely she hadn't planned this three years ago.

"Bad people do things sometimes that shock us." Owen eased down onto a stool. "I do believe, unfortunately, that we should start digging even deeper into Isla's background, with the idea that she is—without doubt—involved, if not spearheading this unfortunate series of events."

"But," Leah countered, "based on the money aspect, for this to work, Raymond has to turn up dead."

Owen nodded. "It's the only way the insurance policy pays out without a long legal battle."

"But those messages and those calls were to his number." Leah didn't get this part at all. "Why would he go along with her plan if the only way for it to work out in an advantageous way was if he was dead? I got the impression he's a very intelligent man. I can't see him being this obtuse."

"She may have used his phone and sent the messages, then deleted them on his end. Accepted the calls and then deleted those. He wouldn't know. Which would mean they had to spend some time together over the time frame the calls were made and the messages sent."

"The police will be able to find out about the calls and text messages without his phone and without that one." She nodded to the burner.

"They will. I'm sure Lambert has already gotten a warrant and requested the records for his phone. Probably for yours and Isla's as well. Those records will show all calls, when and where they were made, and the duration. As for text messages, in some cases the content of recent text messages can be obtained. There's every reason to believe they will have all we saw on the burner available via Douglas's phone records. The burner phone may not have your name or any other attached to it, but its location at the time of a call or text will be available. If a call or text was sent from the vicinity of your apartment, for example, that information will be provided in the call record."

Leah understood. "In that case, in order to point to me, the calls and messages would have needed to originate from our apartment or the library where I work."

He nodded. "Or wherever you were at the time. If the mastermind behind this setup is as good as I suspect she or he is, then every aspect of the pieces of the puzzle will have been carefully thought out."

The ability to breathe escaped Leah temporarily. She would be a fool not to realize that would be the case. So far the whole sham had been very carefully orchestrated. There was no reason to believe this part would be any different.

"What can we do?" Tears burned in her eyes, even though she was suddenly fighting mad.

"How good is your relationship with your boss?"

The question surprised her. "At the library?" He nodded, and she shrugged. "Fine, I guess. I mean, she probably isn't really happy with me right now, since I haven't been at work in several days. But I called and explained the situation."

Owen picked up the burner phone and shut it off. "We have a small window of time, I suspect, before the call records for Douglas's phone make their way to Lambert. If he links that burner phone to you, I have a feeling he's going to want to start moving toward making an arrest. You have no family in the city, no permanent ties like a house or a business, which makes you a flight risk."

Leah's breath caught. "How do we prevent that from happening?"

"We prove that you weren't the only person who may have sent those calls and those text messages."

"Makes sense, but how do we do that?"

"If the library has security cameras, we talk to your boss. See if we can find Isla in the library or nearby, outside the library during the times the calls or text messages were made. If the time frames match up, then we can show doubt at the idea that only you could have sent them."

Anticipation fired in Leah's veins. "There are cameras. Two in the library and at least two outside."

"Tomorrow morning," he said, "we go to the library and see what we can find. For now, we put the phone up and don't think about it."

That would be about as easy as having teeth pulled without a numbing agent. "I can try," she admitted.

Owen suddenly reached for his own cell and checked the screen. "I need to take this."

Though there had been no ring, evidently he had gotten a call. Probably had his phone set to silent. Leah watched as he walked out into the back courtyard. She imagined it was a call from one of his colleagues at the agency. Could be a girlfriend or wife. She hadn't noticed a wedding band. They hadn't discussed his personal life. Part of her was disappointed at the idea that he might be married or involved with someone. It was ridiculous, but just about every aspect of her life right now was ridiculous. What was one more?

Her mind kept going back to the idea that her friend—her best friend—could be responsible for all this. Why would Isla do such a thing? Leah had never once sensed that Isla was not honest with her or that she was only pretending to be her friend.

But then, Leah had never been particularly good at spotting duplicity. Look at how deeply she'd gotten involved with Chris before the trouble started. She'd had no idea just how far into the drug world he had been. She had ignored the rumors, too besotted to believe her parents or anyone else.

She had been a fool.

Had she been a fool with Isla too? With Raymond? The possibility that Raymond had misled her was far easier to swallow. They barely knew each other. But Isla...that was immensely difficult to fathom.

Yet the evidence kept pointing in that very direction.

Then again, the evidence regarding Raymond's disappearance led directly to Leah, and it certainly was not true.

Maybe Isla was a victim too.

But how had that phone gotten into Leah's room?

Owen came back into the house. "That was Jamie."

Jamie Colby. Not just a colleague. The head of the agency's granddaughter—someone high up the food chain. Leah's heart nearly stopped. "Is everything okay?" If there was an emergency and Owen had to be replaced on her investigation, she might just break down and cry like a baby.

"It's about the Chris Painter case."

If he had told her it was about Santa Claus, she wouldn't have been more shocked. "Are you serious? What about it?"

"Apparently, he has been found right here in Chicago."

Something like an earthquake shuddered through Leah. "Are you saying they found his body?" If that old case somehow got tangled up with this new one... Oh God, surely that wasn't possible.

"No," Owen said, his expression serious, his gaze searching hers. "He's alive. He claims to have been held prisoner here in Chicago all this time."

"Prisoner?" Leah didn't know what to say. This was surreal. She wasn't sure how many more revelations she could handle.

"He walked into the Fourth District precinct two hours ago. He's at Northwestern Memorial Hospital, being evaluated. What we know so far is that he is dehydrated and malnourished."

This was impossible. Leah couldn't grasp the ramifications... It was unbelievable.

"Walker here."

Leah's attention jerked back to Owen. He'd gotten another call. She tried to breathe, but the air just wasn't making it to her lungs. Chris was alive? He'd been alive all this time? Who had held him prisoner? And how ironic that he would be in Chicago as well. Or that he would be found in the middle of this other mess.

She closed her eyes, tried to slow the spiraling thoughts. The whole situation was outrageous and growing more so every minute.

"Leah."

She forced her eyes open and met Owen's gaze. The worry there almost undid her completely. If this latest news had him worried…she was doomed.

"Detective Lambert has asked that we come to his office in the morning at ten."

She moistened her lips. "Did he say why?"

"They found Douglas's body."

Chapter Eight

Wednesday, August 13
Colby Agency Safe House
East Elm Street, 8:00 a.m.

Owen had gotten up early for a conference call with Victoria and agency attorney Alfred Mannington. One of the agency's top criminal attorneys, Darren Brocato, had sat in on the call and provided the best advice for Owen going forward. If Lambert chose to move toward an arrest or even suggested as much at this time, Brocato would act as Leah's representative if she accepted the offer. Once the call ended and Owen heard Leah moving about upstairs, he started breakfast.

The toast popped up and Owen added it to the plates he'd prepared. Scrambled eggs, fresh fruit and toast. He was no master chef, but he made a mean scrambled egg. The secret was adding a little milk when whisking. He would let Leah be her own judge. It was doubtful that she would complain, even if she didn't like his efforts. She was too kind. He still found it difficult to conceive that she'd been involved with someone like Chris Painter as a senior in high school. He'd done his research on the guy. Painter and his crew had been serious trouble. Not to mention the thirty-year-old man, now forty, had been way too old to be dating a high schooler. Maybe not by legal standards, but in Owen's opinion.

Just then, Leah walked into the kitchen. "Coffee smells great." She mustered up a smile that didn't reach her eyes. "Good morning."

Assuredly, the effort wasn't one of her real smiles. He'd gotten a glimpse of the real thing a few times. Her whole face came to life with one of her genuine efforts. This one was nervous and for his benefit only. Not to mention her voice was a little over-bright. She was trying but couldn't quite pull off the *I'm okay* mask. She had every right to be nervous. The situation for her grew more complicated each day, as well as admittedly more disturbing.

"Good morning." He gestured to the plates he'd finished preparing. "This is my limited breakfast endeavor." He chuckled. "Hopefully, it's edible. If you like butter or jam on your toast, there's a nice variety available." The staff who maintained the safe houses were particularly good at stocking kitchens when guests were expected.

Her smile widened a bit, the expression prompting a little extra light in her eyes this time. "Looks great. Thank you for going to so much trouble."

They ate for a while without talking. He had spent a good deal of time last night considering how the setup mounting around her appeared to be a bit of an overkill. The end game seemed fairly clear at this point, and still the hits kept coming. This newest element—the resurrection of Chris Painter—really was over-the-top. Last night they hadn't talked a lot about that news or even the more painful reality that Raymond Douglas's body had been discovered. Leah had called it a night quite early. Owen understood she'd needed time alone to think.

She managed a few bites of eggs and half a piece of toast before diving into the questions he'd fully expected this morning. Her gaze fixed on Owen's. "Where did they find him? Raymond, I mean."

"They weren't liberal with the details," he clarified. "But it was near the lake house. In a car registered to him."

She nodded slowly. "No sign of Isla?"

"There was no mention of her." He understood the question she really wanted to ask but dreaded the answer even more than the previous two.

She sipped her coffee, then cleared her throat. "How..." Deep breath. "How did he die?"

This was where things got even stranger and considerably more murky. "He was shot, once, in the chest."

Another slow nod. "I guess that's where all the blood in the lake house came from."

The answer was not as cut and dry as that, and he only knew the few details at his disposal because the agency had friends in the medical examiner's office. Certainly Lambert had not shared the gritty details as of yet. The detective was far too convinced Leah was his best potential suspect.

"There's some question about that, actually," he explained, pushing his plate aside as well. He didn't look forward to relaying the rest to her. She was already hurt at the prospect of how she'd been fooled.

Her gaze searched his. "What do you mean?"

"The amount of blood found in the lake house was enough to suggest he died there," he explained, "but what the medical examiner found when examining the body was that the injury sustained with the gunshot would likely have caused far more internal bleeding versus external. The large amount found— outside his body, obviously— at the lake house is not consistent with his injury."

"Then the blood wasn't his?" Doubt and uncertainty clouded her expression.

"Testing confirmed the blood was his. The consensus we—meaning my colleagues from the agency and I—reached was that the blood was taken as if he'd given blood, like a donor, and then it was used to establish the appearance that he had died in that bedroom."

"Like the book *Gone Girl*," she suggested.

"Exactly like that, yes," he agreed. "But he was killed somewhere else by that single shot. What will help clear you of involvement is to know the actual time of death."

Sharing the other details wasn't exactly breakfast conversation, but she needed to hear the rest.

"The ME determined that the body was in the vehicle for some time before it was found. With temperatures in the high eighties, the heat inside the car sped up the decomp process and created some difficulty in determining a precise time of death, but the ME assigned to the case is very good. He'll pinpoint it as closely as possible. Obviously, the timing will not fit with you being the one who killed him, since many witnesses—employees of the Chop House—saw him, alive and well, around midnight on Saturday."

She considered all he'd said for a few beats, then asked, "Was there a head injury?" She touched her temple. "That's where the blood I saw was coming from when he was being dragged on that kitchen floor."

"No head injury. I specifically asked that question in the conference call with Victoria. Not even a scratch."

Leah digested this detail for a time. "So the blood I saw may have been planted to make me believe he was injured."

"Quite possibly."

Something changed in her demeanor. Her shoulders straightened; her lips set in a firm line. She was angry. Understandably so.

"Then it's true." Her words were edged with ice. "Raymond was part of whatever this scheme is to set me up. Most likely Isla, too, since the lake house belongs to her and her mother."

"There is good reason to believe as much, yes." Sugarcoating the situation or trying to lessen the blow at this point would be ridiculous. Her longtime friend was no doubt involved. He supposed it was still possible that she was a victim as well, but the idea seemed increasingly unlikely.

"I contacted her brother this morning."

Leah stared at him expectantly.

"He hasn't heard from her in years. Or their mother. There was a falling-out about six years ago. He was quite put out that I would even call him, and he wanted me to 'lose' his number."

"Wow. She mentioned they didn't keep in touch. But she never said a word about a falling-out at that level. Good grief, all she did was lie to me." Leah poked at the scrambled eggs with her fork. Took a bite and chewed far longer than necessary. "Is there any suggestion that some aspect of this is related to Chris?" She shook her head. "I mean, I don't see how that's possible. What happened with Chris was a long time ago—before I moved to Chicago or even knew Isla and Raymond."

"I can't answer that question," Owen admitted. "We don't have enough information to hazard a guess. We will, in time, find those answers for you."

"I can't keep waiting for answers." She moistened her lips. "I need to see him." She nodded as if only now, after saying the words, attempting to convince herself of the strategy. "I have a right to know why he left me to deal with all the fallout nine plus years ago. If we wait, some of the thugs he wronged will come after him, and then I may never know the truth."

Although Owen understood her reasoning, he couldn't help wondering if she wanted to see Painter because she still had feelings for the man. He had been her first love... Maybe on some level she was still in love with him. But then, that was none of his business unless it somehow affected the investigation. He understood this, but accepting it was a different story...for reasons completely unreasonable and inappropriate. Other investigators had told him about developing feelings for clients—some even married those clients—but Owen had not encountered that issue...until now.

Clearing his head of the thoughts, he opted to chalk her question up to mere curiosity whether it was precisely true. He liked Leah. More than he should, really. He'd felt a subtle attraction to her the moment they met. But being attracted to his client was not smart under the circumstances—never was, actually. Someone had gone to a lot of trouble to set her up, and he needed to find the reason and determine all the players involved. Hopefully to stop that person or persons and to see that Leah was not falsely accused or harmed.

"I understand," he said in response to her statement, "you feel the need for closure or perhaps for some sense of peace about what happened with Painter. But we need to proceed with caution when it comes to his sudden reappearance. We have no sense of his intent where you're concerned. At this point it's not clear if he was held against his will or if he was in hiding and is now pretending to have been a prisoner." Owen might be guessing on that aspect, but it was a valid possibility.

"You're right, of course." She frowned, then nodded as if needing to convince herself. "I would very much like to have some sort of closure, but until we understand how this happened at this particular time, I agree that it's not a good idea to barge into the situation." She scoffed. "After all these years and all I went through, I feel like punching him in the face…or worse. Still, I really am worried that the ones he double-crossed will show up. His friends were not the type to forget, much less forgive. Not that he deserved to be forgiven."

Owen smiled. "I would suggest that you not comment on your personal feelings when the reporters and Lambert start throwing questions at you."

She laughed. "I assure you, I will not comment."

The sound of her laugh made him smile. "Good."

"You cooked," she said, standing, "I'll clean up."

"I'll help," he insisted. It would give him something to do other than watch her.

For a while, they worked without speaking. The sound of clattering dishes and running water filled the silence. But there were things he wanted to know about her.

Things that had nothing to do with the investigation. He ignored the urge for as long as possible.

"You must love reading," he commented.

She looked up at him, her hands sudsy. "I do." She shrugged and turned her attention back to the task of scrubbing the pan he'd used. "There was a time when I thought I would be a writer." She laughed and shook her head. "I was going to write the next great American novel. But I quickly realized I am not a writer. I love books and I love reading, but I'll leave the creating to those born with the talent."

The change of subject lightened the mood considerably. He confessed, "I don't always have as much time to devote to reading as I'd like, but I do enjoy a good mystery from time to time."

"Mysteries, romance... I love it all. My hope is to prompt that love in my students. Sometimes all it takes is reading the right book to ignite that love."

"I'm sure you'll be a great teacher."

She passed the pan to him and stared out the window, her hands resting on the counter since there was nothing more to wash. "That's if I get through this mess without ending up in prison."

He set the pan aside and put his hand on hers, gave it a squeeze. "The Colby Agency is not going to let that happen."

She turned her hand up and entwined her fingers with his, her gaze searching his face before settling on his eyes. "Thank you. I can't imagine going through this without you. And the agency," she hastened to add.

He managed a smile, when what he really wanted to do was lean down and kiss her. He sensed that she badly needed to be kissed. "I am really grateful I was the one chosen to help."

As if she, too, felt that sizzle of attraction, her gaze dropped to his lips. But then she looked away. "I should get prepared for the meeting with Detective Lambert."

Her fingers slid from his, and she hurried away, disappearing up the stairs.

He finished in the kitchen, taking his time in an effort to distract himself.

Whatever Lambert and his team had found that they hadn't shared so far, Owen was determined to keep Leah safe and ensure she walked away from this situation unscathed. He didn't have to wonder whether she was innocent. His instincts had never steered him wrong, and he was one hundred percent certain she was the victim in this twisty business of betrayal.

He suspected they might never know all the details unless they found Isla Morris alive.

But that was the problem. At this point, with Douglas dead...the prospect of finding her alive was growing dimmer and dimmer.

Chicago Police Department
Addison Street, 10:10 a.m.

LEAH REMINDED HERSELF to breathe calmly, evenly, though it was immensely difficult to do either. Panic nipped at her, wanted to rise and spread through her, but she fought it. This was no time for a panic attack. She'd had a few in her life, and she certainly did not want to deal with that right now.

Owen sat beside her. He was calm and steady, the very

things she needed to be. In truth, he was the one part in all this that prevented her from losing it completely. The reality of what someone had done to her was shattering.

As soon as they had arrived at the department—five minutes before the designated time—they were escorted to a conference room. Leah couldn't decide whether that was good or bad. Were they meeting with others besides Lambert? Owen had warned her not to talk or ask questions about the case while they waited. Lambert or one of his colleagues could be listening.

Not that Leah had anything to hide. She was innocent in this bizarre chain of events. Her supposed best friend, it now seemed, had set Leah up for her own personal gain. Although she couldn't see how Isla would be gaining anything—her name wasn't on that insurance policy. Leah was one of the beneficiaries. If she were charged with Raymond's murder, it was unlikely she would receive a dime.

So how did Isla expect to gain anything? Certainly Raymond Douglas wasn't going to.

Leah and Owen had not spoken in depth about this aspect of the case. She guessed he didn't want to go there until they had further confirmation that Isla was involved. He likely wanted to spare Leah's feelings. At this point, she was so far beyond being upset that her longtime friend may have betrayed her that she wasn't sure she could get past it even if it turned out Isla wasn't involved.

The door abruptly opened, and Detective Lambert walked in. He closed it behind him, so evidently this meeting would be only the three of them. Leah relaxed just a little. Maybe this wasn't as bad as she had feared.

Then again, assuming anything could be a mistake. This eerie situation had taken several unexpected twists.

"Good morning." Lambert sat down, his attention fixed on the open file folder in his hands. "Thank you for coming."

"Good morning," Owen said. "I would hope that by now you will have found the necessary evidence to clear Ms. Gerard."

Leah stared at the man next to her a moment, hoped to God he was right. Then her attention swung back to the other man—the one who held all the cards, or so it seemed.

Lambert fixed his attention on her. "Your prints were found in the lake house. In several rooms." He said this without preamble or explanation of why he thought the find was relevant.

"We were there," Owen said. "We're the ones who found the blood and called you. This was Leah's first visit to the lake house. I would think that the number of prints found that matched hers was few, no matter how many rooms were involved."

Lambert stared at Owen for a moment before turning back to Leah. "Mrs. Morris stated that you had been to the lake house many times with her daughter, Isla."

"That is not true," Leah responded. Owen had suggested she not answer any questions unless it was something very straightforward that they had already discussed. This one—a comment, actually—fit those parameters. He also warned her not to expand upon the most direct answer.

"You're saying," Lambert pressed, "that Mrs. Morris lied in her official statement."

"What Ms. Gerard is saying," Owen countered, "is that Mrs. Morris has never personally witnessed Ms. Gerard at the lake house. Her statement on the matter is mere hearsay."

Exactly. Leah managed a deep breath. She was so glad she had been smart and let Owen answer that one. She would never have been able to come across so emphatic and logical. All the more reason she was incredibly thankful for this man.

She stared at him now. Maybe more than she should admit.

Lambert considered the open file in front of him once more. Leah wished she could read the words and clearly see the images on the pages, but she could only make out enough to be worried all the more. This thing just kept expanding.

"In your statement," the detective said as he lifted his gaze to Leah, interrupting her worrisome thoughts, "from the incident at the restaurant, you said Raymond Douglas was being dragged across the floor and that there was blood on his temple, as if he had sustained a head injury."

"Yes." Leah bit her lips together to prevent saying more.

"Why couldn't you see who was dragging him? That person was surely taller than the stainless steel table that blocked Douglas from view once he was pulled fully behind it."

Leah waited for Owen to answer that one. She glanced at him. His full attention rested on the detective; the stony set of his jaw warned that he was losing patience.

"I visited the restaurant and viewed the window through which she witnessed the events that occurred in the kitchen that night," Owen said. "The only way to see between the two tables that stood perhaps eight feet apart was to be looking straight through the window in that swinging door. On the other hand, the only way to see the person dragging Mr. Douglas would have been for her to step to her right and lean against the door."

Leah nodded as he spoke. He was right. The view she'd had was limited, not only by the small size of the window but also by the shelving units flanking the door on the kitchen side. The window was designed to alert anyone approaching the door of someone about to push through it, not to provide a wide-angle view into the kitchen.

"My guess," Owen went on, "is that the reason she did not do this was because, obviously, she was in shock. It's a perfectly logical reaction. She saw Douglas on the floor, bleeding, and then his body being dragged along. It's human nature to stare at something so surprising or shocking for a few seconds to ensure that you are indeed seeing what you believe you are seeing. Then another moment is required to react. By that time, the person pulling the victim would have been blocked from view by the stainless steel shelving unit loaded with pots and pans and other cooking related items next to the tables. I'm sure you noticed this as well, if you had a close look at the scene."

Leah had not really thought about any of it at the time. She had been too busy staring at Raymond, unconscious or dead, on the floor. For several seconds she had been certain she was imagining it. She hadn't even thought to look at who was pulling him—if she could have seen him or her. Once she realized it was actually happening, her only thought—the one pounding in her brain—had been to run for her life...and call the police.

The detective looked from Owen to Leah. "The medical examiner has tentatively called time of death at some point on Monday. In the afternoon, he suspects. But there is a good deal more work to be done in order to narrow down that time frame."

His words echoed over and over in her brain before she could react. "Then you know it wasn't me," she said before she analyzed the prudence in doing so. Lambert had mentioned he had someone watching her after she went home Sunday morning. No doubt she was watched until she went to the safe house with Owen on Tuesday.

"In addition to watching Ms. Gerard," Owen said, "I'm confident you've monitored the location of her cell phone."

"We're aware," Lambert admitted, "that you did not murder Raymond Douglas."

The words struck Leah like a tidal wave washing over the shore. Finally. Did this mean the truth was emerging? She wanted to be relieved, yet she knew there was a *but* coming. She could hear it in his words, see it in his face.

"However, we still have questions as to whether you and your roommate have been working together. Planned and executed the event. Perhaps Isla decided to double-cross you, Leah. Have you considered this? It would be to your advantage to tell me all you know, and perhaps there would be a deal for you."

Every ounce of strength she possessed was required to prevent responding to that statement with all the fury building inside her. She wanted to shout her indignation, to rant at him for wasting time by being focused on her.

Instead, she deferred to Owen. He would know how to best react to the man's ridiculous suggestion.

"In any scenario you can concoct," Owen began, "how would Ms. Gerard's participation in the murder of Raymond Douglas be believable, considering she would have known that the insurance policy would scream her guilt? You must be aware by now that she is a victim in this scam as well."

Lambert scrubbed a hand over his jaw. He looked from Owen to Leah. "Not once in three years did you suspect your roommate was some sort of scam artist?"

Leah shook her head. "Never. Honestly, I can't believe she would do this. Isla is brilliant. She's going to be a doctor. Why would she throw it all away—even for five million dollars—when she has so much future potential to lose? I'm confident her lifetime income potential is far more than that amount. She's young, with her entire life ahead of her. Think of all that would mean she was throwing away."

It simply did not make sense. Who would do such a thing?

Big exhale from Lambert. "The answer is quite simple. Because your roommate is not a student in medical school or anywhere else. Not legally."

Leah drew back at his words as if he'd slapped her. "What are you talking about? Isla is in her final year of medical school. I've watched her studying. Her schedule is insane."

"Isla Morris was a medical student, yes," Lambert confirmed. "But your roommate and Isla Morris are not the same person."

Shock shimmered through Leah, rocking her to the

very core of her being. She somehow managed to turn her head and exchange a glance with Owen. Judging by the expression on his face, he was more than a little surprised as well.

Owen shifted his attention to the detective. "The agency confirmed the roommate's attendance at Northwestern as well as her employment at the hospital."

"Whoever this woman—your roommate—is," Lambert said to Leah, "she is not Isla Morris." He shifted his focus to Owen. "I have reason to believe the woman who invited Leah to move in with her is Alyssa Jones, and has been pretending to be Morris for just over three years."

"We'll need more details," Owen said, visibly unconvinced.

Leah couldn't speak. Her mind was still reeling.

"Isla Morris and Alyssa Jones were friends. They looked so much alike they could have been twins—even her mother said so. Olive, Isla's real mother, cremated her daughter after her tragic suicide three and a half years ago. In her grief, she foolishly allowed this Alyssa Jones to come and go in her home at will. She saw Alyssa as a sort of second daughter and firmly believed she could trust her completely. After Isla's death, she clung to Alyssa. Depended on her. Alyssa seemed to be a godsend."

Leah couldn't believe what she was hearing. Just when she thought this situation could not get any more bizarre. "You are absolutely certain this person I've known all this time is not Isla Morris? The woman I've met who gave us the key to the lake house is not her mother?"

"Correct," Lambert confirmed. "In fact, the woman you met who posed as Isla's mother has vanished. Her home looks as if it was ransacked and abandoned. We're still trying to identify her."

"I'm somewhat baffled," Owen admitted. "My agency found nothing in Isla Morris's background to suggest she was deceased. I'm aware the department has its resources, but none better than ours. Where is your in-depth knowledge coming from?"

"Frankly, I was confused myself when this thing with Douglas started," Lambert confessed. "You see, my wife and Olive Morris were friends back in high school. They hadn't seen each other in years, but when Isla died, Olive was devastated. She called my wife and begged her to persuade me to look into the girl's death because Olive was convinced her daughter wouldn't commit suicide. I conducted an unofficial investigation of sorts. Followed up on the coroner's report, that sort of thing."

He exhaled a weary breath. "And I spoke at length with the friend, Alyssa. She insisted the intense pressure Isla was under at school had her on edge. She went into great detail about the anxiety and other issues Isla hadn't told her mother about. She was so sincere. Damned persuasive. I bought the story hook, line and sinker. So you see, the mistake was mine."

"But you didn't say anything," Leah said, bewildered and feeling more hurt than ever. "You questioned me repeatedly, and you said nothing." He'd made her feel like a criminal!

"When I interviewed you," he explained, "early Sunday morning, I was stunned to discover that Isla's identity had been stolen. But I needed to let this thing play out in hopes of discovering the whole truth. I believe Alyssa Jones took over everything for Olive after Isla's death. Olive went into seclusion. Didn't talk to anyone. Didn't hold a memorial service for her daughter. She just stopped caring about anything, which likely left Jones with free rein...until she had everything she wanted. Birth certificate, family photos, money...whatever. If I'd had any doubts about my conclusion, those were gone when I checked with the medical examiner's office and no file for Isla Morris was found. This woman—Alyssa Jones, aka Isla Morris—may or may not be a professional, but she orchestrated the takeover of Isla's life like a professional."

Owen shifted in his chair, the move drawing Leah's attention. He asked, "Why are you telling us this now?"

Lambert studied Owen a moment, then looked to Leah. "I'm telling you this, and I shouldn't. If my commander learns about my personal involvement in the case, he'll take me off this investigation. I need to find the truth. I owe it to Isla and her mother. If you will work with me—play along—we may be able to draw this Alyssa Jones or whoever she is out of hiding."

Leah shifted her attention to Owen. "I would really like to help."

Owen nodded, then said to Lambert, "We'll need more information about what you have planned. Starting with, where is the real Mrs. Morris?"

Lambert's expression grew even more somber. "You have no idea how much I wish I could answer that question. I've gone to her home and gotten no answer. Her neighbors say they haven't seen her in ages." He shrugged. "I may have had a look around in her home, unofficially, and all appeared to be just as it should be. So, to answer your question, I have no idea."

"What is it that you expect of my client?" Owen prompted.

"Well, my official reason for calling you here today," Lambert said to Leah, "was to let you know that you're no longer a person of interest in the death of Raymond Douglas. I'll keep working the case, but I fear I won't find the answers I'm looking for without your help." He shifted to Owen then. "If you can protect Ms. Gerard, I believe I can draw out this Alyssa Jones, or whoever she is—bear in mind that according to all our databases, she does not exist. Anyway, I fear this is the only way I'm going to learn what has happened to Olive Morris. I'll start with a press briefing to tell the world that Douglas's body has been found and Leah Gerard is innocent of his murder."

Owen nodded. "This will lead the roommate to believe the life insurance will pay off. She'll be watching Ms. Gerard."

"Yes." Lambert nodded, his expression hopeful. "I believe this was her intent all along." He glanced at Leah. "But I worry that I can't prove it without your help."

Leah looked to Owen and nodded. She wanted to help. The person she had trusted the past three years had betrayed her and likely had plans to kill her. Leah wanted to see her go down, and anything she could do toward that end was fine by her. All she needed was for Owen to have her back.

"We can work with you on this," Owen agreed. "But we'll need assistance with another matter."

Lambert's expression turned guarded. "I'm listening."

"Chris Painter has resurfaced, and Ms. Gerard needs details. Perhaps even a visit with the man. It's my understanding the Chicago PD has him under guard at the hospital."

Lambert considered the request while Leah's heart thumped harder and harder.

Finally, he said, "I think I can arrange that."

Owen looked to Leah; she nodded again, then he turned back to Lambert. "Then we have a deal."

In light of the fact that Leah was now officially cleared of suspicion, she should have been happy. But what she felt was betrayed, used…and terrified—terrified that what she would learn would be far worse than what she already knew.

Terrified that Chris Painter would tell her secret.

Chapter Nine

Gerard/Morris Apartment
Chestnut Street, 1:00 p.m.

The press conference hit all the local stations.

Leah had been bursting with the need to do something since leaving the meeting with Detective Lambert. He'd asked her to return to the apartment she had shared with the woman who had called herself Isla Morris, and tomorrow she was to go back to work. She had done as Lambert asked and worked it out with her boss to have the evening shift tomorrow, which would include closing up the library. Bolling, the building manager, had ensured the apartment was ready. It was almost as if the explosion never happened, except every now and then, Leah got a whiff of a smoky odor. She supposed it lingered in places that were difficult to clean.

Lambert had made an official call to Isla's brother to inform him that his sister was deceased and his mother was missing. But the man hadn't wanted to hear it. He'd been just as curt and uncaring with the detective as he'd been when Owen called him. Leah wanted to judge him for the behavior, but honestly how could she? After what she'd done to her family, she had no right to judge anyone. No matter that she'd straightened up...she had hurt them badly.

Leah turned off the television and crossed her arms before turning to Owen. "Is waiting all we can do?"

He was so still and quiet sometimes. She couldn't help wondering what he was thinking. Maybe she didn't want to know.

"We've done a great deal already," Owen reminded her. He sat on the corner of the sofa back. "We changed the passwords on all your bank, credit card and other personal accounts. Same with the social media accounts. If Jones attempts to gain access to one of your accounts, she'll have no choice but to come directly to you."

This was true, but those efforts felt like nothing that was moving the investigation forward. As difficult as it had been to suffer through seventy-two hours of being made to feel as if she had committed some horrible crime, having to wait for the real person responsible for all this insanity to reappear was even harder. Maybe only because Leah had lost her patience already. Her entire life had been turned upside down, and now all she wanted to do was get this behind her. This wasn't the first time she'd had to right her life, but she sure hoped it would be the last.

"I know." She exhaled a big breath. "It's just hard to stand around here and wait." She had kept her life so carefully organized and in control for the past few years, to live with this uncertainty and total loss of control now was not easy.

She walked over to the window and scanned the street in search of the black sedan. It hadn't reappeared after Owen had lost it on their last trip to the safe house. And it certainly wasn't anyone Lambert had scheduled to keep her under surveillance. If the unknown surveillant had seen the detective's press conference, he would surely expect her to end up back at this apartment.

The Colby Agency was still working on tracking down his identity. The license plate had been traced to a leasing company. The car had been leased by one of Raymond Douglas's businesses, but the driver who'd picked up the vehicle had used a stolen ID. False identities seemed to be a theme in all this.

Leah had called first thing that morning and checked on her mother. She didn't generally allow three days to go by without talking to her mom, but this had been a week of doing things out of the ordinary, and any and all schedules had gone out the window. But Leah hadn't mentioned any of that to her mother. No need to worry her. There was nothing she could do, and upsetting her would not have helped.

"She went with me to see my mother once," Leah said, the memory only then occurring to her. Cold flowed through her veins at the thought. She turned back to the man watching her. "What if this Alyssa goes there and tries to hurt or use my mother in some way?" She should have thought of that possibility before. Her mother had no idea about any of this. Maybe Leah should have warned her about the pretend Isla. All her mother had ever heard was good things about Leah's roommate.

"We have eyes on the facility," Owen said as he walked toward her, then surveyed the street beyond the window. "She's not getting to your mother."

Relief washed over her, making her knees weak. "Thank you. I really should have considered the possibility as soon as Detective Lambert told us about Isla... Alyssa." She scrubbed at her forehead. "I don't know where my brain is."

"We should get out of here. Go to a restaurant you and your roommate patronized regularly. Maybe later tonight, go to a club or other social gathering spot the two of you frequented. Being seen out will lend credibility to Lambert's plan."

He was right. "Okay. That's a great idea. We should go to Tempo. It's—*was* our favorite place. We'd walk there all the time for pancakes or burgers. I think we've probably tried everything on the menu at one time or another."

"Let's go, then. It's a nice day for a drive."

"Tempo is just up the block and across the street. We can walk."

He smiled. "Even better."

As they left the apartment building, Leah couldn't help feeling as if someone was watching. By the time they were on the sidewalk, she had shaken the feeling off. There was no sign of the black sedan. No reason, she supposed, for the police to still be monitoring her activities. Unless they hoped Alyssa would make a move to interact somehow with Leah. With effort, she forced the thoughts away and focused on the moment.

This tree-lined block was one of the reasons she had been so thrilled when the offer to share the apartment came along. She'd struggled so hard those first two years in Chicago to keep a decent roof over her head. Isla—she gave herself a mental shake; not Isla, Alyssa—had been a godsend. How could someone who had seemed so nice, so helpful, have been such a bad person? How could she be heartless enough to wreck someone else's life to get what she wanted? Not to mention a cold-blooded killer? It just didn't fit with the woman Leah knew. Then, on top of that, was the time period. They had been roommates for three years. Had Leah just been in the wrong place at the wrong time on Saturday night? Surely the plan had not been scheduled for three years. Maybe the friendship had been real in the beginning...until Alyssa Jones needed a scapegoat.

Any other idea made no sense. Whatever the case, obviously Alyssa had been instrumental in setting up Saturday night's fiasco.

Leah drew in a lungful of air, reminding herself to focus on the now. It was a little warm today, but the sun and the light breeze felt great.

"This was a good idea." She glanced up at Owen. "Thanks for suggesting it."

"You've been cooped up at one place or the other since this thing began. It's nice to get out." He smiled. "To think about other things."

That smile of his made her feel lighter. She focused forward. Getting too attached was a bad idea. Though they'd only been together for a few days, she felt so comfortable with him. More at ease than with any guy she had dated. This was the absolute wrong path for her thoughts. She felt confident his suggestion to think about other things was not that she should be thinking about him. Oh well, she couldn't turn it off with him right beside her, looking so handsome in his navy trousers and that sky blue shirt that highlighted his eyes. And smelling so...so good.

Maybe the distraction was sheer desperation or necessity, but it felt nice anyway.

As they approached the intersection of West Chestnut

and North State Street, the towering buildings edged out everything else. The trees disappeared, save for the small ones sprouting from carefully planned squares of earth revealed along the sidewalks. Traffic lights and streetlamps took the place of the larger trees. The narrow, barely two-lane side street became a wide city passageway with turning lanes and crosswalks and ever-present traffic.

"Just on that corner." She pointed to Tempo. The lovely one-story painted building with its arched natural-wood windows was neatly tucked in amid the towering skyscrapers. The petite structure sat on the corner, the East Chestnut side flanked by an outdoor-dining space.

This was another one of the things Leah had enjoyed about living at Chestnut Place. There were so many shops and restaurants within a short walk. The hum of the city energized her. She refused to allow the betrayal of the past few days to take that away from her. This was home, and no one was robbing her of that feeling.

She would just have to see about taking over the lease and getting herself a new, trustworthy roommate.

They passed Leah's favorite coffee shop. She and Isla—Alyssa—had been there together many, many times.

A sickening sensation settled in her stomach when she considered how thoroughly she had been fooled. Pushing the thought away, she smiled and thanked Owen when he opened the door to Tempo. The café wasn't so busy, since the lunch crowd had diminished. Getting a table and ordering was quick.

Once the waitress had taken their order and drifted away, Owen asked, "Have you given any thought to where you go from here?" His blue eyes searched her face as she scrambled to figure out how to answer his question, since she really had no idea. "I mean, I'm sure you'll be finishing at the university. But will you be staying in the same apartment, or do you feel a change is in order?"

"Good question." She hadn't gotten that far with any sort of plan. "The lease has *her* name on it, so I'll have to see how or if I can change that."

"I imagine the rent is fairly steep for a student with only a part-time job."

"I have some savings." Actually, what she had was the remainder of the trust her father had left her. Not exactly enough, but something. But she really wanted to save that for anything her mom might need. "I would probably need to find another roommate."

She'd used the larger portion of her trust for her mother, and she did not regret doing so. With her whole heart, she was confident her father had expected his wife to be well cared for. The problem was, he hadn't noticed that the payment information hadn't been updated on the life insurance policy he'd purchase years ago to take care of her if something happened to him. In part, Leah had blamed the life insurance company for not trying to call a longtime customer, but there was no changing that sad fact once her father was gone. Instead, the policy had lapsed, and there was nothing for her mother. The savings her father had accumulated had already been established as a trust for Leah. He'd changed their will and set up the trust since, at the time, their only daughter had appeared determined to screw up her life. The trust only allowed for the withdrawal of a certain amount each year. Except for medical needs—which was how she had managed to use the money at a faster pace for her mother's needs.

"I have a friend," he said, "who owns a building not so far from where you live now who has great studios for really good prices. I can put in a word, if a move to something smaller and less expensive would help."

"I should do that," she agreed with a resounding nod. "The idea of looking for a roommate is..." She made a face. "Not something I really want to do."

"Understandable. I'll give my friend a call. We can go have a look when you're ready."

We. A rush of warmth gave her goose bumps. The very best part of this conversation was the idea that he anticipated seeing her even after this investigation was finished. As foolish as it sounded since she hardly knew him, she really hoped that was a possibility. Maybe it was the hero-worship thing, but it felt like something more.

"Thank you." She smiled. "I really appreciate everything you're doing."

The smile he flashed back at her made her heart beat even faster. She really had to slow down. She was getting far too accustomed to having this man around.

They both ordered a cheeseburger and fries, which hit the spot. Leah added a vanilla milkshake to hers. She hadn't inhaled that many carbs in a while, and she desperately needed the boost they provided—however temporary.

Maybe it was all the sugar from that milkshake, but the words were out of her mouth before she could stop them: "Do you have siblings?"

She instantly bit her lip. In all the discussions about

her personal life, he had never once offered any details of his own. Maybe it wasn't allowed. Whatever the case, the question was out there now.

"Two sisters," he said without hesitation. "Both older. I've spent my entire life being bossed around by them."

Leah laughed. "I thought you were going to say *protecting them* or *scaring off boyfriends*."

"That too," he admitted. "But mostly I've always done whatever they asked. Lauren got married three years ago and has the first grandchild on the way. Madilyn is engaged. But both still call me first when they're worried."

A smile tugged at her lips. "I love that they respect your input so much."

He inclined his head toward one shoulder. "Lauren is a psychologist, and she has told me many times that I'm far too calm and steady for a man just turned thirty-two. Madilyn insists that I take after our mother, and the wild child that never developed will appear when I least expect it."

"I'm not sure I want to know what that means." Leah grinned when he turned up his hands. "Wait, yes, I have to hear it!"

"The story goes," he explained, "my mother and father married very young—which is true. She was eighteen and he was twenty and still in college. By the time Mother was twenty-five, she had three kids. Our father had graduated by then and was working as an engineer in a coveted government position. So all was good financially. But then, at thirty, Mother suddenly experienced an early midlife crisis and took off for Paris."

Leah's jaw dropped. "Paris as in France?"

He nodded. "She said she'd never gone to Paris the way she always wanted. Father was forever too tied up at work to take any real time off, so she decided to just do it alone. She landed in Paris and then spent fourteen days traveling around Europe as if she hadn't a care or an obligation in the world. Both grandmothers were appropriately appalled and came to take care of the children. For the three of us, it was like a trip to Disney World. The grandmothers spoiled us entirely during her absence. On day fifteen in Europe, Mother woke up, spent the whole day in tears and trying to get the fastest flight back home."

"What a story." Leah grabbed another french fry from her plate. "What happened when she got back?"

"Father apologized for ignoring her and promised it would never happen again, and just like that, life returned to normal, except for one thing." He held up one finger. "From that point on, no matter how busy work got, we took a real family vacation every year, and each year on their anniversary, our parents took a mini vacation, just the two of them, to wherever Mother wanted to go."

"I love it! Your family sounds wonderful." Leah supposed the way she had pined for siblings her whole life made her more vulnerable to someone like the roommate who had misled her so completely. Or maybe she just wanted to believe such a cool relationship could be real. Either way, she yearned for those close attachments. Too bad she'd always chosen the wrong people to form attachments to.

"I'm certain they would adore you," he said. "Both sisters and my mother are avid readers. You would have much in common."

Another stream of warmth filled Leah at the possibility of meeting his family. She smiled, though her lips tried hard not to shake with uncertainty. "I'd love to meet them one day."

His smile slipped and he reached for his cell phone. He looked at Leah. "It's Detective Lambert."

Leah held her breath.

Owen took the call but didn't put it on speaker since they were in a restaurant. He made several comments, but none that provided any inkling as to what Lambert was saying. When he finally ended the call, Leah found herself holding her breath once more.

"Two things." He pressed his lips together for a moment as if he wasn't looking forward to the necessary share. "The body of the real Isla Morris's mother was found in a freezer in the basement of the Morris home. It will take some time before the ME can determine cause of death."

The possibility that the woman Leah had trusted killed the poor woman tore at her like the claws of a rabid bear. "This just gets worse." She blinked back the tears of regret and frustration. "I'm afraid to ask what the second thing is."

"If you still want to see Painter," he said, obviously no happier about this part, "Lambert has made the arrangements."

The warmth Leah had been enjoying while listening to Owen talk about his family vanished. A cold flood of defeat and fear replaced it.

Another person was dead. And then there was the other. She didn't want to see Chris…but she had to.

Northwestern Memorial Hospital
East Huron Street, 3:30 p.m.

A UNIFORMED POLICE OFFICER stood outside the hospital room.

Owen showed his ID, and the officer nodded. "Detective Lambert gave approval for the two of you to go in."

Owen looked to Leah. "Do you want me to go in with you?"

She chewed her lower lip a moment before forcing the words from her mouth. "I should do this alone." She didn't want to do it alone, but she couldn't be sure what Chris would say... Oh God, how had she allowed her life to end up at this place?

So damned screwed up! She'd spent all these years pretending this day would never come. But here it was.

Owen nodded. "I'll be right here if you need me."

Leah resisted the urge to hug him. She wasn't sure there was a way to ever properly show her gratitude. This decision to see Chris alone, she hoped, would not make Owen doubt how much she trusted and appreciated him.

Still, this private meeting was necessary.

Leah took a breath and stepped up to the door. The officer opened it and she went inside.

The first thing to hit her senses was the beeping from the machines monitoring the patient's vitals. The lights in the room were dimmed a little. Then her attention settled on the bed. A sheet covered his body from the waist down. He wore a faded blue hospital gown. Since the gown had very short sleeves, it was easy to see that his arms were no longer the thick, muscular ones from all those years ago. The tattoos that had impressed her as a teenager had faded and shriveled to the point of being unrecognizable. But it was his face that really startled her. He looked far older than he had back then. A scruffy beard covered his jaws and chin. His blond hair was darker than before and on the stringy side. His closed eyes were sunken, leaving his cheekbones jutting out painfully.

This looked nothing like the guy she'd fallen so hard for. But then, she had been a kid. Barely eighteen. She had been desperate for excitement.

She had been immature and incredibly foolish.

Slowly, she approached his bedside. His arms lay alongside his torso, his left arm clustered with IVs and a blood pressure cuff.

She placed her hands on the bed rail and considered what to say. Maybe nothing. He seemed to be asleep. But then, she might never get this chance again. Alone, anyway.

His eyes fluttered open, taking the decision out of her hands.

Deep breath. "Hello, Chris."

She wondered if he recognized her. Her hair was the same—same color, same length—and she was basically the same size. But she was older. Tired from juggling work and school, and from dealing with the strange things that had occurred this week.

She had gone from witness to a crime to a murder suspect to…whatever Lambert saw her as now in the space of four days.

"Leah."

A too-familiar sensation flickered through her. The way he said her name was the same. She had loved hearing her name on his lips. He was her first love, her first lover. She would have done anything for him.

And then he'd disappeared, leaving her heartbroken and alone and in the crosshairs of pure evil.

"You're alive," she decided to say. "Everyone thought you were dead."

He managed a small smile. It wasn't until then that she noticed his cracked lips. "That was sort of the point, apparently."

Part of her still wanted to punch him, but he looked to be in no condition to absorb the blow. "You double-crossed the wrong person." It was what everyone assumed. And it was true.

"I sure as hell did." He made a rusty sound that may have been an attempt at a laugh. "I guess I, as they say, got too big for my britches, and it cost me more than I was prepared to pay."

Now she was just flat-out pissed. "You?" She leaned forward to ensure he heard her words. "The man whose money and drugs you stole was going to kill me."

"But he didn't." His jaw hardened, lips formed a thin line.

"No." All the emotions she had expected to feel if she ever saw Chris again were missing. All she felt was empty, sad. "He didn't because I gave him what he wanted."

"Yeah, I heard."

"Are you going to tell?" The one thing she didn't want to feel—fear—crept up her spine.

He stared at her for a long time before he answered. Each second that ticked off made that fear climb a little higher, until it coiled around her throat.

"No. What happened was my fault. I screwed up. I left

you and the others to suffer the consequences. You did what you had to. Who am I to judge?"

Surprise radiated through her. She had. It had taken getting a beating like she'd never experienced in her entire life, but she'd spilled her guts in the end. "How did you get away?"

"He's dead—the one who held me captive all this time. His latest wife said she didn't want to take care of me, so she let me go."

"You killed him?" Leah wasn't sure she really wanted to hear the answer.

He moved his head slowly from side to side. "Nah, he had a heart attack—at least, that's what the wife said. Since she was the only one to give him a kid, she was expecting to get all his money and to take over the business. But she didn't want to deal with me, so she smuggled me out of his compound. First thing I heard when I got out was the trouble you were in. I figured the quickest way to find out about you was to turn myself in."

"Why didn't you just take off and keep going? I doubt anyone is even looking for you anymore." He wasn't making sense.

"I didn't want to leave Chicago until I knew you were okay. I figured I owed you that much. As it turns out, the only person who had anything on me is dead now. The feds wanted to question me, and I saw an opportunity, so I gave them an earful. They'll be taking me away as soon as I'm on my feet again. Witness Protection. I'll be starting over somewhere. A house, a job. I'll be set."

"Good for you." Leah meant it. "Perez held you prisoner this whole time?"

Lorenzo Perez had been a big fish in the world of

drugs. Leah really was surprised he hadn't executed Chris. Her, too, for that matter.

"He said keeping me prisoner was worse than killing me, and at first he was right. But the more time that passed, the more lax he grew with his punishments. Eventually, it was just like being stuck in a really bad motel with an old friend who visited occasionally to brag about his exploits."

Leah laughed, couldn't help herself. "Only you could survive more than nine years of being held hostage by an infamous drug lord."

"My old man always said I could talk my way out of most anything." He looked away for a moment. "I'm sorry, Leah, for what I did to you. I hope you can forgive me."

"It doesn't matter anymore. You didn't do anything that I didn't let you do. Since I'm the one who told Lorenzo where he would probably find you, I suppose we're even…mostly."

She would never be even with her father's death, but that one was on her, not Chris.

"Guess so," he agreed.

"Well." She squared her shoulders, dropped her hands to her sides. "I should go."

"Take care of yourself, Leah. Make good choices."

She laughed. "You too."

She left knowing without a doubt that only one of them would make good choices. The possibility that Chris would be happy on the straight and narrow was highly unlikely.

Leah, on the other hand, was never looking back, and she would do everything in her power to make the very best choices possible.

Chapter Ten

Gerard/Morris Apartment
Chestnut Drive, 8:00 p.m.

Owen couldn't help wondering, even hours later, what Leah and Painter had talked about. The meeting had only lasted seven minutes. Yes, he had ticked off every second in his head.

This case—this *woman*—had totally undone him on some level. He had been with the agency for ten years. He'd started fresh out of university. He'd spent the first four years in research. Then, six years ago, Victoria had asked him to become a field investigator. To say he'd been pleased would be a vast understatement. He'd completed the additional training and took on his first case six months later.

In all the intervening time, he had never once been physically attracted to a client. But Leah…he felt protective of her—sort of the way he felt about his sisters, but not in a sisterly way at all.

His phone buzzed, and he retrieved it from his hip pocket. Ian Michaels, one of Victoria's closest colleagues and a former US marshal, had responded to Owen's request for information.

According to Ian's contact, Painter would be moving into the Witness Protection Program. Although Lorenzo Perez was dead, Painter had considerable and quite valuable information about his network. Once word got out that he had cooperated with the authorities, he wouldn't be intruding into Leah's life again—not if he wanted to stay alive.

Another text message appeared, this one from Lambert. He had four members of his team in place at the Underground, Leah and Owen's destination for the evening. She and the woman who called herself Isla Morris had frequented the dance club over the years. No one expected Alyssa Jones to be hanging out there, but someone who knew her and who was there may have seen her since Saturday night. Leah was acquainted with most of her former roommate's friends. She had some idea of the faces to look for.

The club was the same place she'd run into Raymond Douglas that one time before the ill-fated date.

"I guess I'm ready."

Owen turned to Leah and for a moment he couldn't speak. Her hair was in a high ponytail, making her look incredibly young. She wore a short denim skirt and a pink scoop-necked tee. Her long legs flowed down to a pair of pink high heels. She…looked…great. And sexy as all get out.

"Wow." He took a breath. "You look very…*prepared*." The only photo he'd seen of her dressed this way was from ten years ago in her senior yearbook. She'd had the yearbook hidden in one of her dresser drawers. When he'd searched her room, he hadn't been able to resist having a look.

"I feel a little ridiculous." She shook her head. "Dressing for a night of clubbing after what's happened."

"Keep in mind it's part of the investigation." He grinned. "And you actually look...great. I like it."

She rolled her eyes. "You look pretty great yourself." Her gaze roved down, then back up his body, the move starting a fire deep in his gut.

"You said very casual. Do I meet the criteria?" He didn't generally wear blue jeans and a T-shirt on the job, but blending in tonight was important. Good thing he always packed a pair of jeans. The Guns N' Roses tee wasn't his; Leah had suggested he wear it. It belonged to her. She used the vintage tee as a nightshirt.

The idea that she'd slept in the tee, no matter when that might have been, had kept him on the edge of arousal for the past hour. Seeing her in that skirt was not helping.

"It's perfect." She gave him a nod. "That tee looks better on you than it ever did on me."

He doubted that was the case. "Thank you. Shall we go?"

She crossed the room, moving slowly, maybe because those heels were so high, or maybe just to make him more... Well, anyway.

"I have one question first." She stopped directly in front of him.

"If I'm lucky," he managed a smile, "I have the answer."

"If we're playing the part of a couple," she began, studying his face as if she expected the answer to appear there, "what exactly does that entail?"

She was going there, was she?

"I would think," he said, searching for the words that

wouldn't sound so inappropriate, "that sticking together in the crowd would be essential."

She nodded. "I can do that." She tilted her head and eyed him expectantly. "Anything else?"

"We could hold hands." He nodded, thinking that was a good idea. Reasonable. Not over the line. "Maybe share a toast at least once."

"What about dancing? I really like to dance."

"Sure." This one was a little more precarious. "Dancing would be expected, considering the venue."

"Okay." She smiled. "I think I've got it."

He was glad, because the way she was looking at him while she asked those questions was making him wild with need.

When had merely listening to a woman talk become such a turn-on?

Maybe it was just something about her…that touch of uncertainty and naivete that seemed absolutely genuine. She might be twenty-eight, but he had a feeling she had been holding herself back for a long while now.

The way she watched him as he locked the apartment door made him wonder if she was having the same trouble he was. If she was ready to let go, he was in trouble.

Then she took off toward the stairs at the end of the corridor, and the way she moved almost finished him off completely.

The Underground
Franklin Street, 10:00 p.m.

FINDING A PARKING SPOT had been an ordeal, but nothing Owen hadn't faced before. Living in the city, sometimes a car was a more of a nuisance than an asset. They had stopped at a favorite restaurant of his in the River North area, the Smith, for dinner. From there, they'd made their way to the club, which included round two of Find a Parking Spot Without Losing His Mind.

He and Leah held hands as they walked from the car to the club entrance. It amazed him how soft her skin felt. Forcing his mind away from the thought to prevent other, more salacious thoughts, he focused on their surroundings.

As the name suggested, the place was underground, in a basement. The style inside was very European. An elevated DJ booth overlooked the dance floor. Tables hugged the walls all the way around the space. The music was loud, and the place literally vibrated with energy. The flashing colored lights kept time with the music.

Not too crowded, but that would change as midnight neared. Leah held on tightly to his hand as she threaded through the crowd in search of an empty table. She found one and moved in for the take. Most of the tables were pub-style and made for standing around. A few had chairs. Those, of course, were all occupied.

A waiter passed and Leah waved him down. "I'd like a vodka on the rocks with lemon." She turned to Owen.

"Whatever you have on draft," he said, loudly enough for the waiter to hear.

The waiter gave a nod and hurried away, weaving effortlessly through the growing crowd.

Leah leaned close and said, "Don't worry, I always nurse a single drink for the entire evening." She made a face. "I'm not much of a drinker, actually."

He'd suspected as much. Anyone who liked a good

stiff drink from time to time would have been doing so after what she'd been through. He hadn't seen her go for so much as a beer. Just the wine that once.

For a while he watched her scan the crowd. Sometimes she stood on her tiptoes as if she needed to see over someone. She was far more relaxed than before. Made sense. She was no longer a murder suspect, and the man from her past who had still been haunting her was accounted for and wouldn't be unexpectedly appearing in her life again. Not if he was smart, anyway. Once they knew who was behind the setup that included her name on an insurance policy, the investigation, from her perspective, would be finished.

Closing a case was a good thing, but somehow this felt not so good.

He rested his crossed arms on the table, primarily to be nearer for conversation purposes. "Spotted anyone you recognize?"

"Not yet." She made a disappointed face.

She turned to him and he realized his mistake. His position put his face level with hers when she looked at him. As hard as he tried not to, he found himself studying her lips.

She smiled and his heart thumped.

"Come on." She grabbed his hand and pulled him away from the table. She wove a path through the crowd with almost as much ease as the waiter.

Their destination appeared to be a table where three women stood huddled together. Just as they reached it, Leah called out, "Maya!"

The other woman turned around and shock showed on

her face for a split second before she dove at Leah, wrapping her in an enthusiastic hug.

"Oh my God." The one Leah had called Maya drew back and looked her over. "Are you all right? I can't believe what I've been seeing on the news. I started to call, but I wasn't sure if I should."

Which was code for *I didn't want to get involved.* Some friend. Owen recalled Leah mentioning that Maya was one of Isla's friends who hadn't really warmed up to her at first.

"It's okay," Leah said, talking loud enough for the other women to hear over the music. "But I'm really worried about Isla. No one has seen her since Saturday. She hasn't shown up for work, and her mother hasn't heard from her either."

Maya's expression turned apprehensive. "Are the police looking for her?"

Leah nodded. "I'm really worried she has...ended up like Raymond."

Maya's hand went to her chest. "No, that can't be. Maybe she's hiding. I can ask around. See if anyone has heard from her."

"That would be very helpful," Leah said. "I need to know she's okay."

Maya nodded, then glanced at Owen.

"Sorry." Leah shook her head. "This is my friend Owen." She turned to Owen. "This is Maya, Isla's friend I was telling you about."

Maya smiled at him, then glanced at Leah. "Where did you find him?" She waggled her eyebrows. "He's hot."

Owen opted to act as if he hadn't heard her comment.

"He's helping with the investigation," Leah explained.

Maya's expression blanked. "Is he a cop?" She stared at Owen with something like fear or uncertainty.

"Not a cop," he explained, leaning closer to ensure she heard him. "I'm a private investigator."

Maya nodded, her expression still obviously uncertain.

"We need to find Isla," he said. "We believe she is in danger and needs our help. If you or any of her other friends sees her, please let her know that we can help."

Maya shifted her attention from Owen to Leah. "Do you really think she's in trouble?"

Leah moved closer to the other woman. "Absolutely. You don't want to know what they did to Raymond. I have to find her and warn her."

Owen had to hand it to her, Leah was playing it just right. He put his arm around her and moved closer into their huddle. "We will make sure she doesn't end up like that poor SOB."

Maya nodded slowly. "I'll get the word out to everyone who knows her." She frowned then. "Are you at the apartment?"

Leah nodded. "Where else would I go?"

"Of course. I don't know what I was thinking." Maya hugged Leah again. "You be careful too. I thought for sure you and Raymond were both done for."

"Me too," Leah admitted. She peered up at Owen. "But I had a secret weapon."

He smiled at her, but the look in her eyes made any amusement her remark had garnered vanish, and something entirely different settled in. Electricity was crackling between them, jumping wildly like the dance floor lights.

Rather than draw back, he kissed her. Slowly, briefly.

The lightest of kisses. But the fire generated from his lips touching hers threatened to burn them both down.

Leah turned fully into him, stretched her arms up around his neck. His went around her waist, and the feel of her body pressing into his had his mouth deepening the kiss.

In the background, he heard Maya say, "See you around," but slowing this kiss down, much less stopping it for anyone, was out of the question.

Leah pulled back, her eyes wide with surprise and no small amount of desire. "We should mingle."

Before her words could filter through the haze of want blinding him to every single thing but her, she had grabbed his hand and was tugging him forward. He followed, struggled to relax the need roaring inside him.

Control...he had to regain control. This thing buzzing between them made doing his job inordinately difficult. He could not compromise her safety...or the case.

For the next half hour, they wandered through the crowd, stopping to dance when a song Leah liked vibrated from the speakers. He spotted at least one of Lambert's people. The guy parked at a table looked far too uptight and watchful to be a regular patron.

By the time Leah announced she was ready to leave, Owen was incredibly grateful. He wasn't sure how much more he could take of this pretending to be a couple without making a serious mistake. His whole body hummed at the sound of her voice, the touch of her hand.

When they emerged onto the sidewalk in the night air, he relaxed marginally, sharpened his focus on their surroundings. A few people strolled the sidewalks on either side of the street. A car—not the black sedan—

rolled slowly past. Lambert had people here. Leah's hand squeezed his, and she glanced up at him with a dreamy smile. This, he decided, was going to be a long night.

She held on to his hand until they were in the car heading back to Chestnut Place.

There was no talking…just the distinct sizzle of electricity still flowing between them. He had maybe fifteen minutes to regain some semblance of control.

*Gerard/Morris Apartment
Chestnut Street, 11:45 p.m.*

LEAH'S FINGERS FUMBLED twice in her effort to unlock the door. Though Owen waited behind her, the smell of his aftershave was driving her mad.

If they hadn't been in the middle of that club, she was certain that kiss would have ended up going way, way further. She had never been kissed like that. Ever. Even now, she could scarcely breathe thinking about it.

The truth was…she had wanted way more than just that kiss. Still did.

Finally, the key turned and the door unlocked. Owen placed a hand on her arm to remind her that he needed to go in first. If anyone was waiting inside, he wanted to be the one at the front of the line.

Leah closed and locked the door behind them and then sagged against it. Her body was on fire. She couldn't even remember the last time she'd had sex, but she wanted it now. Wanted it in the worst way.

When he was about to head into the hall toward the bedrooms, she couldn't take it anymore. "Wait."

He turned around, worry in his expression.

She pushed off the door she'd just locked, let her purse drop to the floor and walked straight up to him. Her arms went around his neck, and she rose onto her tiptoes until her lips locked with his. He hesitated, let her do what she would without reacting, which only made her more desperate. Her fingers threaded through his dark hair, her breasts rubbed against his chest—sending fire shooting straight through her.

Finally, his arms went around her and he pulled her tightly against him. She made a sound of want, and he reacted, lifting her off her feet and moving toward the bedroom. Her legs went around his waist, and he staggered to a stop, pressed her against the nearest wall. He glided one hand over her thigh, moving toward her bottom. She cried out. He deepened the kiss. She nipped his lower lip, and he repaid her in kind.

He lifted her away from the wall and moved through the door to her room. She wanted to rip that T-shirt off his body...wanted to feel his skin beneath her palms. When he reached the bed, her feet dropped to the floor and her hands went instantly to that tee, tugging it out from his jeans. He removed his belt, all the while kissing her.

They were doing this...yes, they were. If he stopped now, she would absolutely die.

His fingers went to her hair and worked the elastic from it, letting it fall around her shoulders. He traced the length of it down her back.

Her own fingers struggled with working his tee upward. His hands moved away from her long enough to pull the wad of cotton over his head and drop it to the floor. Her hands went instantly to his chest, glided over his skin...feeling the heat and the pounding of his heart.

Her tee came off next, and then he was easing her down onto the bed. She relaxed into the softness of the covers, and he climbed on top of her, his knees on either side of her hips, keeping his weight off her body.

But she wanted to feel the weight of him...she wanted to...

Her elbow brushed against something cool on the covers. She froze.

"You okay?" he whispered breathlessly.

"There's..." She tried to reach whatever it was with her hand but couldn't get in the right position. "There's something in the bed."

He was off her instantly and yanking her up and away from any potential threat. The bedside lamp suddenly came on, and she blinked her eyes to adjust to the light.

A faceted heart-shaped glass object sparkled red against the white covers. Another smaller piece, and then another and another, spread out around it. Leah rushed to her bedroom window and opened the curtains she kept pulled across it.

"The wind chime." She walked back to the bed and turned on the lamp that sat on the opposite side of where she slept. There was enough light then to see the near-invisible strings that connected all the pieces of colored glass. "It hangs in my window." She glanced back at the window, then at the bed once more. "It was in the window when I closed the curtains to get dressed before we left for the club."

"Where did the wind chime come from?" Owen asked.

"Isla—Alyssa. She gave it to me my first Christmas here."

Their gazes collided.

"She was here." His words echoed the thought that had just entered Leah's mind.

"Does the wind chime carry some particular significance?" he asked, not waiting for her confirmation.

Leah shook her head slowly, racked her brain—the one that was still whirling with desire. "No... I..." She thought of the day they'd bought it. A few days before Christmas, at the artisans' market. "We were shopping at that craft market on Ravenswood. I saw it and fell in love. She bought it and said it was an early Christmas present."

"Is the market open now—in August, I mean?"

Leah shook her head. "It's a seasonal thing. It probably won't open until October."

"But you know the place," he said.

She nodded. "We can go there in the morning." Leah stared at the wind chime for a moment before turning back to him. "Do you think she's trying to lure me into a trap? Or send me a message?"

He reached for the tee she had torn off him. "Either one is possible. We'll need to be careful." He handed it to her. "Thanks for lending me the shirt."

She hugged it to her chest. Felt the warmth of his body that lingered in the fabric. "You're welcome. Thanks for helping me get word to her friends that we're looking for her." There was so much more she wanted to say, but instead, she asked, "Can we not tell Detective Lambert about this until we see what it means?"

"If that's what you want."

"I do." She looked away for a moment before meeting his gaze once more. "I'm sorry. I guess I got a little carried away tonight."

He reached out, swiped his thumb across her cheek.

She leaned into his touch, wanting more, but it was his eyes and that smile that made her hungry to pick up where they had left off.

"If you're agreeable, we can do this again...soon," he promised.

"I am most agreeable."

He smiled. "Good."

When he'd left the room, she drifted to her bathroom and washed her face, then brushed her teeth. Instead of wondering what her lying roommate had in store for her now, she couldn't stop thinking about how it felt to be in Owen's arms. And those kisses. Mercy, the man knew how to kiss.

She tugged on the tee she'd lent him, reveled in the smell of him that had permeated the fabric. Next time, she was not stopping for anything. When she climbed into bed, she hugged herself and thought of how it felt to hug him, to slide her hand over all that muscled terrain.

The idea that he was so nice made her smile. The last time she'd been so taken with a man, he had been a total thug. She shook off thoughts of Chris and how old and weak he had looked in that hospital bed. No matter how he'd gotten himself where he was, she couldn't help feeling sad for him. He could have done so much more with his life. But what happened to him wasn't her fault. If Perez hadn't gotten the truth out of her, he would have gotten it out of someone else. All these years, she had felt guilty about telling Perez that it was Chris who had taken his money and drugs. But now she finally understood that none of that was her fault.

The alarm icon on the digital clock that stood on the bedside table dragged her from the past. The time was correct and wasn't blinking, so the power hadn't gone off. But she never used that clock for an alarm. Her phone was her alarm for everything. She sat up and checked the settings. The alarm had been set for ten in the morning. What in the world?

Then she smiled. She understood now. This was Isla's way of telling her what time to come.

Then her smile faded. Not Isla. A liar. A betrayer. Possibly a murderer.

Leah would see her at ten, and then she would have answers, one way or another.

Chapter Eleven

Thursday, August 14
The Raven Artisans Market
Ravenswood Drive, 9:55 a.m.

As certain as Leah had been about last night and what she and Owen had shared—those amazing kisses and, frankly, almost sex—the harsh light of day had her second-guessing herself.

He probably thought her a fool. Really, she was a cliché. A woman in jeopardy, falling for her protector. How sad was that?

The idea had prevented her from fully meeting his gaze that morning. He'd made toast—cheese toast and cinnamon toast. She'd forced herself to eat a slice. Not that it wasn't tasty—it was—but she just couldn't get any more down. She felt sick with regret for her actions. She was attracted to him, but she should have waited until this was done. Then, if they were both still interested... She had to stop thinking about it.

Not that she wanted to regret a moment of any part of their time together—and really, she didn't. She only regretted how foolish she probably looked. Detective Lambert had just told her she was no longer a suspect in

Raymond's murder. Chris had let her off the hook after all these years. She should have behaved more like someone thankful for her freedom from accusation...not a lonely woman who had gone without a lover's attention for far too long.

She dropped her head against the car seat and fought the urge to groan. Instead, she stared out at the empty space that, in a couple of months, would be filled with artisans selling their wares and people excited to explore the many offerings.

Owen had parked very close to the entrance of the large warehouse where the market she had visited with her roommate was held. There was not a single other vehicle anywhere along the street. He had backed into a slot against the tree line opposite the row of warehouses.

"There's no need to regret anything about last night."

The sound of his voice filled the car, wrapped around her and made her want to reach out to him. Another groan rose inside her, but she tamped it back. How was she supposed to think clearly? And why was she so transparent?

"It's not necessary," he added.

She turned her head, met his gaze and her determination to be stronger melted. "I feel like I came off as a little too needy." She might as well be honest. She'd had enough lies for several lifetimes.

He smiled. "We were both a bit needy, but that's human, isn't it? We have needs, and sometimes, when we've ignored them for too long, they come on a little strong."

His words made so much sense. "I..." She swallowed back the doubt. "I enjoyed the *us* part of last night. I know it wasn't real, just part of this thing." She stared forward once more. "But I enjoyed being with you...like that."

He placed his open hand, palm up, on the console. "I very much enjoyed the *us* part as well, and it was very real."

She stared at his hand...his long fingers. She placed her hand there, their fingers entwined. Warmth spread through her, and her smile widened. "I slept in that tee you wore."

He smiled. "I'll hold on to that image, if you don't mind."

"I don't mind." She returned the smile.

They both looked forward then. Maybe to prevent the kiss that would no doubt have happened next. Even Leah understood this was not the time to get distracted. Focus. It was necessary.

The minutes slipped past, and she tried to think of something more to say. It was midmorning, and it was already hot. No, she wasn't bringing up the weather.

"I haven't noticed that black car again." Now, *that* seemed like an appropriate topic.

"Maybe because Lambert's people have been around. Since the detective doesn't know about this morning's rendezvous, it's possible our elusive follower will make an appearance." He turned to her then. "All the more reason to be extra careful."

She nodded. "Okay." The area was deserted. They were flanked by trees on one side and a long row of warehouse-type buildings—most of which were either closed at this hour or deserted for the summer—on the other.

"I keep asking myself," Leah said, the recurring thought suddenly pushing to the front of her mind, "if Raymond was a part of this in the beginning."

"How do you mean?"

She wished she knew. "I mean, he didn't die in the kitchen on Saturday night. According to the medical examiner, he likely didn't die until late on Monday. I'm aware that he may have been held hostage until then, but the part that makes me question his innocence on any level is that when I saw him being dragged away...his eyes were open and there was blood on his temple. If he was alive and unconscious, why were his eyes open? If he was knocked out, why was there no head injury the blood could have come from?"

"You make an excellent point," Owen agreed. "If he was a cooperating party, then perhaps your former roommate will know since she helped to set up the date. And we can't forget that he added you as a beneficiary to his life insurance policy."

Somehow she kept trying to block that part. "You're right. There's really no way he wasn't part of this well before Saturday night." Leah exhaled a frustrated breath. "It's ridiculous, I know, but I don't want to not be angry with *her*. A part of me wants to believe she would never do this. I mean, I've known her for three years. We lived together. I just can't see her doing this. Yet it appears to be the only logical explanation."

Owen turned to her. "Sometimes there is no logic to be found. Particularly if the action involved a strong emotion, like jealousy or revenge...maybe anger."

Another thought occurred to Leah. "Is it possible that Raymond figured out Isla wasn't really Isla? Maybe he was blackmailing her—forcing her to participate. That is motive, and it's oddly logical."

"I've considered that as well," Owen agreed. "Whatever drove her, whatever part she played, I believe it's imperative that we proceed with caution. If she feels cornered or that you represent a threat, your safety could be in jeopardy, and she certainly won't talk to us under those circumstances."

Leah recognized he was right. Whatever she thought she knew about her roommate, all bets were off at this point. She couldn't trust her.

Alyssa Jones, aka Isla Morris, suddenly appeared behind the gate that led into the alley between two of the buildings. Leah's breath caught. She forced herself to raise her hand and wave.

"That's her," Leah said, though she imagined Owen was well aware.

Isla—Alyssa—stood so still, her coal-black hair hanging around her shoulders, her pale skin a sharp contrast to the black tee and slacks. Leah felt at once thankful she was alive and furious that she was.

"Remember what I said," he warned. "Caution is essential."

Leah nodded as she reached for her door.

She and Owen emerged from the car simultaneously. Even from across the street, Leah noted the change in the other woman's demeanor. She hadn't expected Leah to have someone with her.

Still, she waited while they crossed the street. Leah had worried that she would take off. The fact that she stayed put sent Leah's pulse racing.

"Who's he?" Alyssa asked as Leah neared the gate.

"He's a private investigator I hired," Leah said, anger suddenly igniting inside her. "I didn't really have a choice, since you set me up the way you did."

Surprise or something on that order flitted across the

other woman's face. "I didn't set you up. I didn't do anything but get dragged into a situation that had nothing to do with me."

Leah scoffed. "I'm the one who was dragged into the situation. The police suspected me of murder!" She shook her head, worked to tamp down her anger before she scared this...this person off. "He's Owen," she said with a jerk of her head toward the man beside her. "He's helping me." She glanced up at him. "He's a friend."

Alyssa scrutinized him through a narrowed gaze. "Are you sure you can trust him?"

Leah laughed. "You're asking me about trust? Seriously? We're friends for three years. Roommates! And the whole time, you were lying. Your name isn't even Isla Morris. You stole a dead woman's identity."

Alyssa looked away then. "We were friends, Isla and I." She met Leah's gaze. "I was part of the janitorial team at the university. I was assigned to the library and the student center. But it was in the library where Isla spent a lot of time studying, and that's where we met. I helped her study sometimes. Eventually, I came to the apartment and helped as well. We were..." She met Leah's gaze again. "We were more than friends."

"Did you kill her too?" Leah demanded, ignoring the softer feelings that attempted to emerge.

"No." Alyssa's eyes were bright with emotion. "I loved her. But she had serious issues. Maybe her mother was in denial, but I believe Isla was bipolar. Rather than get the help she needed, she and her mother pretended the problem wasn't real. She wanted Isla to stay focused on school—to ignore her needs. Those last few months, Isla was miserable. She didn't want her life anymore. I tried to help, but it wasn't enough. I found her at the lake house. She had taken a whole bottle of her mother's sleeping pills. The next thing I knew, her mother had cremated her and gone into solitude."

"Did you kill her mother?" Leah demanded.

Alyssa rolled her eyes. "No. She took the same way out her daughter did. OD'd on her own medicine."

"So you, Alyssa Jones, put her mother in the freezer and stole the daughter's life."

She shook her head. "Maybe that was part of it, but mostly I wanted to *finish* her life. I wanted to keep her alive, and the only way to do that was to become her and to become the good person she was. Isla kept to herself —because of the disease, I think—so I made new friends for both of us, and I helped you because it was something Isla would have done." She shrugged. "Her mother never closed up her apartment or anything. Never ended her enrollment at the university. As far as I know, she never even notified anyone. They had no other close family other than that scumbag brother. It was just the two of them. There had to be a reason that happened."

Leah turned away, couldn't bear to look at her.

"How did you become acquainted with Raymond Douglas?" Owen asked, speaking for the first time.

Alyssa glared at Owen as if he were her enemy. Leah wanted to be furious with her. To hate her. But how could she, after hearing that story? Then again, maybe this woman was a master manipulator. A liar. A cheat. How could Leah believe anything she said?

Alyssa shrugged. "He was freshly divorced and hanging out at the same clubs as me and my friends. He was quite wealthy, had the right personality. I was drawn to him."

"You were drawn to him, or to his money?" Leah snapped. Those flashes of anger just wouldn't be tamped down.

Her former roommate looked at her, pain in her expression. "I guess I was his type and he was mine. He flirted and I flirted back. But—" she looked at Leah as she told her the rest "—the chemistry fizzled quickly. We saw each other from time to time to blow off steam. But that was it." She drew in a deep breath. "Until a few weeks ago. He said he needed to disappear. He wouldn't say why. But he had a plan, he just needed a witness to…" Another big breath. "To his murder. Then he would disappear and never be bothered again. He gave me five thousand dollars. I needed the money. The funds Isla left in her account were running out, and I was getting desperate. I was never able to access the mother's money."

"He wanted a reliable witness," Owen said, "to his fake murder. Did he ask for Leah by name?"

Alyssa looked away a long moment, then nodded. "He'd looked into the backgrounds of my closest friends, and he thought the problem Leah had that summer after her high school graduation would be useful. It would lend credibility to what he needed the police to believe."

Leah's breath caught. "You told him?" She had shared her deepest secrets with this woman. How could she? Right. Of course. She did whatever was most beneficial to her.

"No," she argued, her fingers curling around the slats of the gate as if they were prison bars, "he found out about it through the background search. I never said a word."

"Doesn't matter," Leah argued. "You still betrayed me."

Her dark eyes shone with emotion. "I did. I'm sorry."

"What went wrong?" Owen asked.

Alyssa blinked, turned her attention to him. "He wanted to stay at the lake house for a couple of days after his fake murder, so I said okay. It wasn't like I needed the place."

"You told the woman pretending to be your mother that you and I went there, but we didn't. Ever."

She looked away. "At first I couldn't face you. That's why I didn't come home on Sunday. I went to the lake house with the intention of telling Raymond that I had to tell you the truth. When I found the blood and the handcuffs, I panicked. I told the woman I hired to play the role of Isla's mother what to say and warned her that she should likely disappear too."

Leah wanted to shake her. "Thanks a lot."

"I knew you'd be okay, Leah," she said, her words urgent. "I never meant for you to get into trouble. I didn't know this was really going down. It was supposed to be insurance fraud, not murder."

If she expected forgiveness, she could forget it.

"Who killed him?" Owen demanded, his tone leaving no room for argument.

"That's the thing, I have no idea. Raymond planned this whole thing himself. I'm pretty sure he didn't tell anyone. He would have been damned stupid to do that. My best guess is that one of the other investors in his business figured out what he was up to and killed him. I really don't know. I just know he said he was in trouble."

"How would this investor know about his plan?" Owen asked. "Or where to find him?"

"I have no idea," she said.

"If you told anyone and caused all this," Leah warned, "you're an accessory to murder."

"No! I didn't. I didn't tell anyone. If you haven't figured it out by now, I'm really good at keeping secrets. Like I said, all I wanted was the five thousand. But then after he disappeared, I was too terrified to talk to anyone."

She shook her head. "But I knew I had to tell you," she said to Leah. "I couldn't have you believing I did this."

Leah met her gaze and lied. "I knew you didn't kill anyone."

Tears welled in her former roommate's eyes. "I'm really sorry this happened. I never meant for it to turn into this."

"What about Douglas's insurance policy?" Owen challenged. "Whose idea was it to put Leah as a beneficiary on his insurance policy?"

Alyssa made a face. "What insurance policy?"

"There is a ten-million-dollar life insurance policy on the man who hired you to help him fake his death," Owen explained. "Half to his ex-wife and half to Leah."

She looked at Leah. "What the hell, Leah?"

A blast of outrage that this supposed friend would dare accuse her roared through Leah. "That's what I've been asking myself all week. What the hell?"

"Are you prepared to turn yourself in to Detective Lambert?" Owen asked. "I'm sure he would be willing to offer some sort of deal for the information you have."

Alyssa drew back a little. "I'm not putting myself in the line of fire when it comes to a murder charge."

"Then help us prove you didn't do it," Owen suggested.

Leah felt like telling him they weren't going to bother,

but that was her anger speaking. "He's with the Colby Agency. If there is anyone who can figure this out, he can. Let him help you."

Alyssa looked from Leah to Owen and back. "I didn't kill anyone. I don't know who did."

"The list of probable suspects is not that long," Owen told her. "You, the ex-wife or the investor you said he screwed over."

Leah wondered if Lambert had even looked at the ex-wife. The investor was a possible lead he might not have known about. But they knew now.

"What am I supposed to call you?" Leah asked before the other woman could comment on Owen's statement.

"Al," she said. "Alyssa Jones is my name, but my mom and the people who used to be my friends called me Al."

Leah nodded. "Did Raymond ever talk about his ex-wife?"

"He never said anything good, that's for sure," she said. "He complained that she was always having her lawyer go to a judge and demanding more child support and alimony. He wanted to be free of her in the worst way."

"Do you know her?" Owen asked. "I would think a person as intelligent as you would have looked into the situation before agreeing to the sort of deal you made with Douglas."

She shrugged. "I did a little checking up on her. Her family was poor. She met Raymond at a nightclub where she worked as a waitress. He always said that once she got her claws into his money, she wasn't letting go. He realized as soon as they had their first kid that he was never getting away from her. She proclaimed right from the beginning that she was never going to be poor again. He says he stuck it out as long as he could for the kids' sakes."

Leah wanted to throw up. What a jerk he'd been. She would never have accepted a date with him if she had known what sort of person he was. "You couldn't have told me this."

Alyssa had no answer, just stared at the ground.

"Did he ever say anything about how far she would go to keep his money?" Owen asked.

The woman shrugged. "All he said was, she would never let go as long as he was alive."

"We need to set up a meeting with Detective Lambert," Owen said. "Will you cooperate?"

Alyssa backed up a step. "I don't think I can do that." She glanced at Leah. "I'm sorry, but this has gone too far. I'm out."

"Please," Leah urged, "your life could be in danger." Maybe she would cooperate if she feared for herself. She certainly cared for no one else. "Someone has been watching me."

"The black sedan," Al suggested.

"Yes." Leah grabbed the bars of the gate. "Do you know who it is?"

She shook her head. "That same car was watching me even before Saturday. I mentioned it to Raymond, and he said it was probably just some guy who had a thing for me, but I knew he was wrong."

"Let us help you," Owen urged.

"I can't." She took off running toward the other end of the alley.

Owen tried to open the gate, but it was locked. "Let's go. We can cut her off on the next block."

They ran to the car and climbed in. He shot out of the parking lot.

When he pulled out his cell phone, she put her hand on his. "Don't call Lambert."

He arrowed her a look. "You sure about that? We can't be certain she was telling the whole truth."

"I know. But we can't be certain she isn't either."

He left the phone on the console and focused on driving. They drove around several blocks but never spotted Alyssa. She was gone.

Leah hoped she stayed safe. As angry as she was at her former roommate for what she had done, she didn't want her to die too.

She just hoped they could both survive this…thing that was still somehow continuing even though Raymond was dead.

Then Alyssa could go to prison and suffer the consequences of her actions.

Leah felt like a seesaw. Up and down… One minute she was up and wanted to believe Alyssa, the next she was down and didn't believe a word she said.

How would they ever find the truth?

Chapter Twelve

Harold Washington Library Center
South State Street, 8:15 p.m.

As long as the weather was good, Leah almost always walked from her apartment to the library. It was a good half-hour stroll, but she enjoyed it. Other times, she took the Blue Line. Walking was her favorite, though. Approaching the iconic brick building with its big old owls always gave her goose bumps. Inside was equally amazing, with ten floors of incredible visuals as well as what you came to a library for—books and research material.

When Leah was offered the position, she'd felt deeply honored. She worked every hour possible between school sessions, and just as many weekends and other odd hours when in session. The past week hadn't worked out so well, but at least she still had a job. She'd worried about the negative publicity related to the investigation.

She'd spent the first half of this evening's shift on the fifth floor, working in the Assistive Resources Center, one of her very favorite things to do when not browsing and working with the books on the seventh floor.

Now she had moved to the Maker Lab on the third floor to do some cleanup after an Open Shop preview class introducing those interested to the array of equipment available, from 3D printers to laser cutters and sewing machines. Such a great opportunity for the community. There was so much offered at this library. Leah never tired of seeing what was happening on any of the floors.

Owen had followed her from floor to floor. He stayed in the background, found something to appear busy, but his attention was always on her. Each time their gazes collided, she shivered.

She tidied the stack of sign-up sheets. Most participants were quite good at cleaning up after themselves, putting away supplies and tossing in the trash what should go there. The Open Shop classes had been fuller than usual tonight. No registration was required for most of them, which allowed bringing a friend at the last minute or opportunities for just showing up when you hadn't been sure you could attend. It was all very relaxed and user-friendly.

Staying busy had helped Leah to put the encounter with Alyssa out of her head for a while. All the things she had said made sense on some level, and yet the idea of trusting her after what she had admittedly done was difficult, at best. The notion of never seeing her again or sharing aspects of their lives was harder than Leah had expected. There she went with the up-and-down thing again.

As promised, Owen hadn't called Detective Lambert about the meeting. They had talked, but he didn't once mention Alyssa. Instead, he asked the detective about Raymond's ex-wife and a potential disgruntled investor. Lambert had, of course, interviewed the ex-wife numerous times. She had an alibi for Saturday night and all day Sunday and Monday. She'd gone to her mother's on Sunday and, after hearing that Raymond was missing, had decided to stay. The children, a fifteen-year-old boy and thirteen-year-old girl, had been with her. The whole thing was horrifying for the children. Leah couldn't imagine anyone hurting a child. Why in the world would Raymond be so uncaring about his own? To have them believe their father had been murdered just to get away from their mother?

It was awful, just awful.

The ex-wife claimed to have no idea about the life insurance policy or any investor problems. Both belonged to Raymond and he didn't share information with her. She did recall that he had taken out the policy a decade ago. She had nothing to do with it. The fact that she was a beneficiary had come as no surprise, but the detail of another woman being on the list of beneficiaries had floored her, according to Lambert. He hadn't given Leah's name, but the news had mentioned her on Tuesday, so the ex knew who Leah was. Leah was immensely grateful she hadn't shown up at the apartment, or here at the library, looking for her.

Mrs. Ward, the personnel director, had assured Leah that she had answered no questions from reporters or anyone else about her. Leah was relieved. The idea that she had been here since two with no lookie-loos or snoopy reporters seemed to back up the director's claim. Security would have escorted them out, but Leah was very thankful it hadn't come to that.

She glanced across the room to where Owen had taken another call. He'd been making and fielding calls all evening. He'd been trying to catch the agent who'd set up the life insurance policy. He was also still digging into the black sedan they, luckily, had not seen today. It was as if the driver had seen all he needed to, and now he was just gone.

Leah picked up a stack of manuals and headed for the storeroom. Each lab shared a very generous-size storeroom with its neighbor. The space was like a Jack-and-Jill, with doors on each end, one to the room where she was just tidying up and another on the opposite end to the neighboring lab. She tucked the manuals onto the proper shelf. Since a few supplies were out of place, she returned them to their correct space. She scanned the room once more, then turned to go. The lights went out.

Leah froze.

There wasn't a timer on the lights... Someone had to have flipped the switch. The silence had her trying to slow her heart's pounding, for fear whoever had turned off the lights would hear it.

Then she ran for the door.

A hard body slammed into her, trapping her against the wall next to the door. She tried to scream, but a gloved hand covered her mouth. He—had to be a man, tall, strong—dragged her backward...across the room and then through the other door into the neighboring lab. She blinked against the light.

He shoved her to the floor. Slammed her head against the hard tile. She tried to scream again, but the next bash of her head made the room spin and her vision darken.

Something wet hit her—her face, her arms—the smell vaguely familiar. Some distant, still-working brain cell had her wishing she could move, but she was fading into nothingness. The sound of Owen's voice calling her name followed her into that black place.

Chicago Hospital
Lawrence Avenue, 11:30 p.m.

SHE HAD A CONCUSSION.

Owen stood at her bedside, his forearms braced on the bed rail. His eyes closed against the images that haunted him each time he thought of what he'd found in the room right next door to where he'd been standing...on the damn phone.

Lambert had called him with the information Owen had asked for. He should have followed Leah into that storeroom while listening to the detective. But he'd been frustrated that Lambert had nothing new on the car, and he'd pushed Owen about where he and Leah had spent their morning. He wasn't buying the excuse that they were just driving around to help Leah relax. She was supposed to be, according to Lambert, searching for her former roommate in places they had frequented—like the club last night.

It wasn't until he'd heard a thumping sound that Owen realized Leah was still in the storeroom. He raced into the storeroom, found it dark but saw the light under the door in the next room. He rushed toward it, burst through the door just in time to see a man wearing a ski mask and holding a lighter. Three things hit him simultaneously: Leah was on the floor. There was a smell...something he had smelled before. And the lighter the masked man held was not the disposable kind but the old-fashioned type that kept its flame once you lit it until you closed the lid to extinguish it.

He charged the guy. The bastard ran, but not before throwing the lighter on the floor.

The instant that lighter flew through the air, Owen's brain identified the odor he'd smelled when he came into the room.

Gasoline...charcoal lighter fluid...something on that order.

Owen dove for Leah. He rolled her as far away from where the lighter hit the floor as possible. Flames lit, searing across the tile floor, then, out of fuel, dying as quickly as they'd started. The fire alarm blared to life.

Leah had moaned and Owen's heart had surged into his throat. He'd used the sleeve of his shirt to wipe the lighter fluid from her face. "Hey, Leah, can you hear me?" he'd asked.

When she hadn't answered, he'd gotten onto his knees and checked her body for injury. No blood. But then his fingers had traced the back of her head, and he felt the lumps there...and the dampness.

He'd sworn repeatedly as he felt for his phone. Where the hell was it? Had he dropped it? He glanced around the room, spotted it.

Scrambling for the phone, he had then recognized the call to Lambert was still connected.

"What's happening?" the detective demanded.

"I need an ambulance. Now!" Owen had roared. "And your people on-site should be watching for a man wearing a ski mask coming out of the library."

Half an hour later, they were in the ER.

The medical staff had removed Leah's clothes, which

had all been doused with lighter fluid, and they'd cleaned her exposed skin. There was some redness, but so far nothing worse. The concussion was a grade 2. The doctor had insisted on keeping her in the hospital overnight even though she'd seemed fine by the time the ambulance arrived at the library. She'd regained consciousness within a minute or so of him finding her, and she'd seemed okay other than being a little dazed and unsteady on her feet.

A few minutes ago, she'd drifted off to sleep. Owen hadn't left her side since he'd found her, other than the time it took for the scan of her brain. And then he'd paced the corridor right outside the room. He just kept thinking of what could have happened if he had not rushed into that room when he did.

A tap on the door preceded Detective Lambert's entrance. He'd been at the hospital when they arrived. As soon as he was satisfied that Leah was okay, he'd returned to the library to oversee the activities there.

"She's asleep," Owen warned, meeting him near the door so as not to disturb Leah. The doctor had said she could sleep as long as she was watched carefully and roused occasionally.

The older man nodded. "No one we interviewed saw a man wearing a ski mask. We're viewing the security video, but we've found nothing on that footage so far."

"He was wearing black," Owen said. "I think the shirt was a button-up, not a tee or sweatshirt. Nothing so casual."

"A lot of people in Chicago wear black, apparently."

If the detective hadn't looked so exhausted, Owen might have snapped at his response, but he cut the man some slack. "Yeah, he probably pulled the ski mask off as soon as he exited the room."

"Strangely enough, the library doesn't have video surveillance on all floors. Just on the main floor and the tenth."

Owen heaved a weary sigh. "Which means we aren't likely to find anything. By the time he got to the first floor, he could have been wearing a different shirt and trousers, for that matter."

"That's exactly what he did," Lambert confirmed. "We found a black shirt and black trousers in a trash bin on the second floor. We've sent both to the lab for analysis."

Which would only help if the guy was in some database. Great.

"This is feeling more and more like a particularly well thought out plan from the beginning." Owen bit his tongue to prevent himself from revealing the details Alyssa had provided that morning.

"My money is on the roommate," Lambert said. "She still hasn't surfaced. She's either dead or is in on it. Maybe both."

"Leah doesn't believe she would kill anyone, but we're both confident she was in on it from the beginning."

"She has had trouble staying within the law off and on for the better part of her life," Lambert explained. "I've gotten access to more records, and it seems her legal issues started early with petty stuff. A woman who would assume someone else's life for three-plus years…" He shrugged. "I don't know. She might be capable of anything." He leaned closer as if to ensure Leah didn't hear this part, although she was asleep. "On the other hand, her GPA is at the top of her class. Keep in mind that she didn't do premed. She took up Isla's life in the first year of medical school. Comments in her file suggest she's some sort of genius. Anyway, there is no doubt in my mind she could pull off this whole scheme. Most of her adult life has been one scheme or the other."

Owen couldn't deny that Lambert had a valid point. The agency had discovered the same about Alyssa Jones. "But we can't be certain about anything. What about the ex-wife? She's the other beneficiary on the insurance policy. Or the investors who may lose money in all this?"

Lambert turned his hands up. "No issues with any investors that we've found so far, and the ex-wife has a firm alibi. Granted, she could have hired someone, but we haven't found the first indication that's the case. She hasn't dated in ages. According to her friends and neighbors, she is completely focused on the kids since Douglas isn't around much."

"Still," Owen argued, "she has the most to gain."

"About the same as Leah, based on the policy," Lambert pointed out.

Another thought occurred to Owen. After the brief meeting with Alyssa, it made the most sense—if anything the woman said was to be believed. "Maybe it is the ex-wife," he suggested. "Maybe she killed him—or hired someone to kill him—for the insurance payoff. And maybe that's why someone has been following Leah and has now officially attempted to kill her."

Realization dawned in the detective's expression. "Because if there are two beneficiaries and one is dead or is convicted in the murder of the insured, the other beneficiary would in all likelihood end up with all the proceeds."

"Leah has already been considered a suspect. It doesn't matter that she was cleared, there have been no other suspects or arrests. The ex-wife would have some legal standing, I imagine, to use that as leverage." Owen considered another thought. "Even if she didn't get the whole payout, maybe it was worth half the policy value to have a scapegoat. Particularly if the goal was to get him out of her life and the lives of her children."

That last part he'd taken from Alyssa's insistence that Douglas wanted his wife out of his life. The feeling was likely mutual.

"I see where you're going. And if the other beneficiary is dead—" Lambert looked to the hospital bed and Leah lying there "—all the better. She gets ten mil. Either way, the ex can walk away clean with five mil. The kids would get anything else he had left."

A sinking feeling tugged at Owen's chest. "Even if the full amount of money doesn't come for years because of the legal issues, it's like money in a trust for the kids. While the ex enjoys the five mil she will get any day now."

"I'll interview her again tomorrow." Lambert pursed his lips for a moment. "If I can get a judge to sign off on it, I'll try for a search warrant of her home. I'll let you know how it goes. Keep me posted on how she's doing." He nodded toward Leah.

Owen assured him he would.

Lambert hesitated before walking out the door. "I've got a uniform outside the door. I'll have another one at her apartment."

Owen nodded. "Thanks."

The detective hesitated once more. "You know, I did finally get Douglas's cell phone records. There were some interesting text exchanges between him and someone using a burner phone. You haven't noticed one of those lying around, have you?"

"Maybe you should check the ex-wife's phone records," Owen suggested, rather than give him a direct answer.

The older man nodded. "On it already."

For a moment after the detective left, Owen stood by the door, staring at Leah in that hospital bed. She looked so pale, so fragile. The IV tube running down to her left arm made his gut clench. He crossed the room, took his place next to her bedside.

He wondered how he could have met her only a few days ago and already feel so close to her...so desperate to know her better, to spend more time with her. To protect her.

Her eyes fluttered open. She frowned, then dredged up a smile. "You look tired."

"Not so much," he lied. "Detective Lambert stopped by again."

"Did they find him?" The fear that lurked in her eyes twisted his insides into knots.

"They're still working on it." But he had a feeling they weren't going to find the guy who had attacked her in the library. Not unless he made one hell of a misstep they didn't know about yet.

"This is just completely out of control." She closed her eyes for a moment. "I do not see how all of this could have evolved from Raymond wanting to make his ex-wife think he was dead."

Owen had been mulling over that scenario as well. He was beating around another theory, but he wasn't sure he wanted to bring it up right now. Leah needed to rest.

"What?" she demanded, then grimaced as if she'd hurt her head by speaking so forcefully.

"You need to rest." The doctor had been clear on how important it was that she rest for a few days.

"Tell me what you know or what you're thinking. I will not rest until you do."

"Alyssa is apparently an expert at assuming identities. She's made up more than one in her life. Have you considered that her knowledge and experience may have been why Raymond asked her for help? If that's the case, then I'm thinking their relationship was something more than she has shared."

Leah appeared to consider the scenario. "It is a big risk, sharing that sort of self-incriminating plan with someone unless you really, really trust them."

"She said she didn't know about the blood or the life insurance policy. But what if she did? What if she killed him for real so she could claim the money?"

Leah's brow furrowed. "How would she claim any of the money?"

"By presenting herself as *you*."

"Except I was a murder suspect—my photo was on the news."

He shrugged. "Granted, that plan backfired, but I'm guessing if it was her, there was a plan B. She's way too smart not to have a plan B."

Leah's expression suggested she was possibly buying into the scenario. "So she would need a way to get the money once it was paid out to me."

The fire in his gut had his instincts on point. This was a very plausible scenario. "I need you to think, Leah. Did you and Alyssa ever discuss your financial situation? Your bank account or savings? Anything along those lines?"

She nodded, her expression clouding with worry. "We talked about everything. She knows where I keep all my passwords, where I bank, how much money I have. Which is why we changed all those passwords," she reminded him.

"Did you ever add her to one of your accounts? You would have to go into the bank, the two of you, to do that."

Leah shook her head. "No. But I do my banking online. She could go on my account from my laptop and transfer money." She groaned. "Because even my new password is saved there."

"Then we can't be sure she isn't waiting around to do that," Owen suggested. "Think about it, she could have disappeared already. The woman pretending to be her mother is long gone. Why is Alyssa hanging around? Why does she care if you believe her? Or if you're still friends?"

Leah moistened her lips. "She wants that five million dollars. At this point, the only way to get it is for her to stay on my good side so I don't change anything that possibly gives her access to it."

"There are things we can do," Owen said gently. "Adding facial recognition to your laptop, for one."

Leah nodded. "Maybe I just need to start over in a new place."

Owen touched her cheek, noted the new bruise there. He winced. "We'll find you a new place where you'll be safe, if that's what you want." Only this time he wasn't thinking of his friend who owned apartment buildings.

"I'll feel a lot safer—" she scooted over to her left a

little, then patted the bed on her right side "—if you're next to me."

"I think I can do that." He lowered the side rail. "At least until a nurse comes in and tells me different."

He stretched out on the bed next to her. Kissed her forehead. "Close your eyes," he murmured. "Rest."

She closed her eyes and snuggled against him. He closed his and considered again how grateful he was that she was okay.

He'd let her down tonight, but that would never happen again.

Chapter Thirteen

Friday, August 15
Bechel's Insurance Company
South Wacker Drive, 11:00 a.m.

The office was a small one. Nothing like Leah had expected, given the building where it was located and the many types of insurance sold. A soaring high-rise made of steel, glass and concrete. The office was on the tenth floor. She read a few of the Google reviews, and there was nothing bad mentioned about the owner or the business, only the surprisingly small office and the idea that it was basically a one-man operation. Owen's research had discovered that the company was actually part of a larger one that had small offices all over the country.

On the elevator ride up to the proper floor, Owen started in again. "You really should be resting in bed or on the sofa watching television."

"You've called this guy three times, and he hasn't called back. It's time for a face-to-face. You said so yourself."

He shot her a sidelong glance. "That was before someone gave you a concussion and tried to set you on fire."

There was that. "We're here." The elevator bumped to a stop, and the doors opened. "We might as well do this."

"Just take it easy," he urged as he waited for her to step into the corridor.

She headed for the office, and Owen followed. He opened the door, and they entered the tiny lobby. There were four chairs, a table with a couple of magazines and a sliding window behind which a receptionist likely sat. But not at the moment. Leah's shoulders sagged. If the man wasn't here, she was going to scream—except that would make her head hurt worse.

Though she would never admit it, she felt exhausted. Irritable. Her head ached. It was all to be expected, but that didn't make functioning any easier. "No one's here," she muttered.

Owen shrugged. "Maybe. We'll just see." He took the three steps across the dinky room and opened the only other door besides the entrance. On the other side was a narrow hall lined with three more doors. The first on the right was open, and it led to the desk behind the sliding window. The one across the hall was open as well and showed off a minuscule powder room.

At the end of the short hallway was the third. Owen glanced at her, held up a hand to knock but then heard a male voice on the other side. Had to be Hoyt Bechel, the owner; otherwise, someone else was using his office.

As Owen prepared to knock again, the man on the other side told someone he would be hearing from him soon and then said goodbye.

When the door didn't open with an exiting client, Owen knocked.

They waited, heard the man on the other side shuffling

around his desk. The door opened and a frazzled-looking middle-aged fellow glared at them through his glasses.

"Can I help you?"

"Mr. Bechel?" Owen asked.

"That's me." He smoothed back the strands of hair that were sticking up as if he'd run his hand through repeatedly.

"I'm Owen Walker. This is Leah Gerard. We're here about the Douglas life insurance policy," he explained. "I've left you several voicemails."

"Ah, yes." He nodded, the movement exaggerated. "Sorry, it's been really busy."

"May we come in?" Leah asked when he made no offer.

"Ah, sure, sure." He backed up, rounded his desk and smiled in welcome. "Come on in and have a seat."

Leah sat down, but Owen remained standing. He braced his hands on the back of the other chair.

"So, how can I help you?" He looked from Leah to Owen and back. "You're one of the beneficiaries," he said to Leah.

"Yes."

"I," Owen interjected, "would like to know how my fiancée ended up being added to this man's insurance policy."

Leah stared at him. His statement startled her, but she recovered quickly. A great cover for the question.

Bechel's eyebrows shot up. "Well, now, I can't tell you the reason, because I have no idea. I met Mr. Douglas a few times. He took out the policy ten years ago. Right here in the office. But when he changed the beneficiaries, he did that online. He ordered a form for updating.

It was mailed to his address of record. He filled it out, signed it and sent it back."

"Was it notarized?" Owen asked.

Bechel shook his head slowly, hesitantly. "We don't require that." He frowned. "If there is some question about whether this was an authorized update by the policy owner, then we'll have to look into it."

"But anyone could have requested the forms as long as they had access to his account," Owen argued.

"Well, I suppose so. But we compared the signatures to the original application. We always do that, and it looked proper. My secretary called to confirm. Those are our safeguards." He turned to Leah then. "I'm sure you're aware there won't be a payout until the homicide investigation is complete. But once all is sorted out, we'll get the money to you."

She held up her hands. "I understand. I'm just trying to figure out how this happened."

"You'll have to overlook my surprise. We rarely have a beneficiary come in with a question like that. Generally, they're very happy to be receiving money."

The man had no idea. "I understand there are two beneficiaries," Leah said. "What happens if one of them dies before the payout? What happens to the money?"

His gaze narrowed. "Well, there are two beneficiaries, and the benefits are fifty-fifty, as specified by the policy owner. If one of the beneficiaries passes away before distribution, the full amount of the policy payout will go to the remaining beneficiary." He held up his hands in surrender fashion. "I'm a little uncomfortable discussing this aspect of the benefits with you. Perhaps we should call Detective Lambert and make him aware of your concerns."

"Detective Lambert is well aware of our concerns," Owen said. "He was at the scene last night when someone made an attempt on Leah's life."

Bechel drew back. "Oh my. This has been a terrible, terrible situation. But I will leave it to the authorities to handle whatever is going on. Please take care of yourself, Ms. Gerard. Rest assured that the underwriters at Patriot Insurance are safeguarding the benefits Mr. Douglas purchased."

Leah stood, her legs a little wobbly. She really did need to rest, but how could she? Someone had tried to kill her, and that someone was still out there!

They were out of the office and back in the elevator, headed down, before she worked up the nerve to say, "I was surprised to hear you'd proposed." She laughed, tapped her temple. "I guess I lost that memory with this concussion."

Owen chuckled. "I thought about it all night while you were lying in that hospital bed."

"You were in that bed with me," she teased.

"This is true." He grinned.

"So you were busy thinking while I was sleeping." Her own grin tugged at her lips.

"It was either that or stare at you, and that may have caused issues."

Leah nodded. "I see."

The elevator stopped and the doors opened.

Owen stepped out first, had a look around and then put her arm in his. "Can I take you back to the apartment now?"

"Not until we see the ex-wife." Leah knew that had been on his to-do list. They needed to stick to the investigation. "I'm fine, really." She was tired, yes. But she could do this. It couldn't wait.

He scanned the sidewalk and street before they exited the building. Once he was satisfied, they began the walk to the car. "Are you certain you're feeling all right? Really."

"Really, I am. I'm a little tired, but that's normal with a concussion like this. As long as I don't try to run a marathon or get into a fight, I think I'm good."

He shook his head. "You are stubborn."

She'd gotten it from her daddy. "I'll rest tonight, I promise."

"You absolutely will," he vowed.

Somehow she had a feeling she was going to really enjoy tonight.

Louise Douglas Residence
Wolcott Avenue, 1:00 p.m.

THE DOUGLAS HOME was a multi-million-dollar residence ensconced comfortably between two other lovely high-end homes. According to Owen's research, Mrs. Douglas got the house and a car in the divorce settlement—as well as a very hefty monthly child support and alimony payment.

City records showed a mortgage on the house. With her ex-husband dead, those big monthly payments would likely be gone as soon as his remaining assets were dissolved or passed on according to his will. The house would be paid off.

Since Mrs. Douglas was a stay-at-home mother, any issues with the estate payout or the insurance proceeds was likely not good. She would need every dime of the five million, plus whatever else there was to inherit in order to maintain her current lifestyle.

A huge motive for murder.

Her ex-husband's and Leah's.

"What if she won't talk to us?" Leah's nerves were jittery.

"Curiosity will force her to talk to us." Owen turned to her. "You ready?"

She exhaled a big breath. "Guess so." She had insisted on doing this, after all.

Owen exited the car and was at her side of the vehicle before she could get the door open and climb out. That was the thing about this concussion. She felt like she was moving in slow motion. Losing time was another thing she'd noticed. Just when she thought five seconds had passed, she realized it was a minute or more.

They walked up the front steps, and Owen rang the bell. The brick-and-limestone house looked very much like a brownstone but was likely only a few years old. It was a style Leah loved, but owning one was about as likely as her winning the lottery.

The door opened, and the woman Leah had seen in photos on Raymond's social media accounts stood before them. Tall, slim, blonde, green eyes and dressed to the nines, as they say. The woman was gorgeous.

"You." She glared at Leah. "How dare you come to my home."

Owen moved closer to Leah as if anticipating throwing himself in front of her. "Mrs. Douglas, we're here to talk about inconsistencies in the events leading up to Raymond's murder. It would be very helpful if you could give us a few minutes of your time."

The fury in her expression made Leah certain she would say no, but then she backed up a step. "Fine. But unless you have something relevant to say, I'm not interested."

Leah relaxed. She tried to see the situation from this woman's perspective. Her ex-husband had been murdered—the father of her children. The source of her income. It could not be easy.

Then again, she was the one with the most to gain from his murder.

For that matter, she may have hired someone to come after Leah. After all, ten million was way better than five.

The entry hall flowed straight to the back of the house, where a large, open room served as a living, dining and kitchen space. It was beautiful, perfect for family living. Whoever designed the home had done a great job.

"Sit if you like," Louise Douglas said as she dropped onto the sofa.

"Let me start," Leah said to Owen. He gave her a nod, and she turned to the ex-wife. "I barely knew Raymond. I met him two weeks ago, just briefly. Then he called and asked me out. I was to meet him at the restaurant Saturday night. That, of course, didn't happen." Leah swallowed, her throat dry. She drew in a breath and went on. "I have no idea why he added me as a beneficiary to his insurance policy. It was totally out of left field and happened before I even knew him."

Louise stared at her for a moment before bursting into laughter. When she'd regained control of herself once more, she swiped at her eyes. "You, that Isla, your roommate, spent endless weekends at that lake house with Raymond. Don't even pretend you didn't know him. Please."

Leah looked at Owen. "I wish I could prove this to you, but I can't. Since we'd barely met, I have nothing to show you or to use as proof. I can only say that I am as stunned as you. In fact..." She probably should have run this part past Owen, but she'd only just thought of it. "I don't want the money. I'll gladly sign whatever necessary to ensure that it all goes to you."

Her gaze narrowed again. "I don't believe you."

"I will." Leah glanced at Owen. He gave no indication that she should stop with this line of discussion. "I can tell Mr. Bechel at the insurance company. I'll tell Detective Lambert. Sign whatever I need to sign."

"I'll have my attorney contact you." Her face warned that she wasn't completely convinced but was willing to see if it worked out.

"Someone," Owen said, "made an attempt on Leah's life last night."

The woman's heavily manicured eyebrows shot upward. "Why bring that up to me?" She glanced at Leah. "You know the saying, 'Live by the sword, die by the sword'? You can't go around sleeping with other women's husbands without finding trouble."

"First," Leah said, angry now, "I wasn't sleeping with anyone. Second, you and Raymond have been divorced for three years."

"I suppose you know the exact date the divorce was final."

"No. But it was part of the research we've done since

the murder. I have a right to look into who might be involved in trying to kill me."

Louise smiled, a vicious expression. "You should probably talk to that roommate of yours. According to my research, she's the ruthless one. I suspect this whole scheme was her idea. It's just the sort of thing she would do to get ahead. Tell me, were the two of you going to split the five million?"

"Leah has already been cleared of any suspicion in Raymond's murder," Owen said. "Your alibi, on the other hand, hinges on your mother's testimony and that of your children."

Fury contorted her face. "Do you think my children would lie for me if I was MIA when their father was murdered? Please."

"I have no idea," Owen said flatly. "Would they?"

She shot to her feet. "I think it's time for you to go. As I told Detective Lambert, if you or the police have anything else to say to me or to ask of me, you can contact my attorney."

Owen stood. Leah did the same. The ex-wife led the way back to the front door. Leah's head was spinning a little. She tried to think of what else she should say, but she really knew nothing relevant to this woman.

At the door, Owen hesitated, one hand on Leah's back, causing her to hesitate as well.

"Are you familiar with a company called After Dark?" he asked. "It's one of your former husband's investments. It appears to be an exclusive catering service."

"I recall some mention of it," she said, "but I'm not really familiar with any of his investments. What of it?"

"There's a black sedan that's been watching Leah. Following us at times. It's leased to that company."

"Knowing Raymond, he failed to follow through with whatever he owed the owner or other investors. Who knows which employee of his or of the business may be using the car?" She sent a look toward Leah. "Perhaps someone who isn't pleased that their boss or investing partner was murdered and who hopes to find the truth."

"Detective Lambert will be contacting you about the car," Owen warned. "Perhaps you'll be able to provide him with more information."

"I'm certain my attorney can answer the detective's questions."

She closed the door behind them.

Leah and Owen didn't speak until they were in the car, driving away.

"She made no bones about showing dislike for her ex-husband," Leah pointed out.

Owen glanced at her. "I'm not sure that *dislike* is a strong enough word."

"All kinds of motive there," Leah said, feeling very tired now.

"She didn't show any surprise when I mentioned the car. She could have someone watching you. But the real question is, did she hire that someone to try and hurt you?"

"What about a boyfriend? She and Raymond have been divorced for three years. Could she have a secret boyfriend working with her?"

"She insisted to Lambert she wasn't dating and there was no one in her life. My research specialist found nothing on her social media accounts or any neighbors who mentioned seeing a frequent male visitor. No black sedan hanging around."

"Maybe she was still in love with Raymond." Didn't seem likely, but who knew?

"Or maybe she just doesn't want the children to know she has a social life. She might be concerned they would tell their father, and that would somehow be a problem for her."

"Possibly," Leah agreed. "She apparently took him back to court a number of times for more money."

"Maybe the money is more important to her than a social life."

"I can see that," Leah agreed.

Louise Douglas was angry and resentful of her husband, but did that mean she wanted to have him killed? Would she have gone that far? Would she have tried to have Leah killed for the other five million? She had seemed startled when Leah offered to turn it over to her.

The woman had suggested Alyssa was at the bottom of all this, but Leah wasn't convinced. Maybe because she didn't want to believe it.

She thought of the way that masked man had beaten her head against the floor and tried to set her on fire.

Would the woman she had believed to be her best friend—like a sister—have hired someone to do such a thing?

No… Leah didn't want to believe that.

But could she really be certain? Of anything or anyone in all this?

She turned to the man driving… She was certain of him. And that was almost worth having to go through this nightmare.

"I think I need to take that rest now."

He glanced at her, concern in his eyes. "Heading that way, then."

Leah relaxed in the seat and closed her eyes. She stopped thinking about all the horrors of the past six days and let her mind wander to those kisses they had shared. And the feel of his strong body next to her last night.

She couldn't imagine a better way to take her mind off all this than doing a little more of exactly that sort of therapy.

Chapter Fourteen

Saturday, August 16
Gerard Apartment
Chestnut Street, 7:00 a.m.

Her cell phone vibrating across the bedside tabletop woke Leah.

She was alone in the bed.

The distant scent of fresh-brewed coffee told her why. Owen was up, had probably been up for a while, making coffee and doing the job of keeping her safe.

She smiled. She'd really enjoyed the gentle way he'd made her feel all sorts of things last night. Safe. Warm. And utterly fulfilled. She couldn't think of any way she would rather spend her nights.

Her smile fell. But what would she do when this was over? Would he go back to his life and forget about her? She'd wanted to ask. While snug in his arms last night, the question had pounded in her brain. Then she'd decided that she would rather just not think about it until she had no choice. Enjoying the moment and the time they had together was more important.

Well, and finding the answers to who had tried to

frame her up for murder—and tried to set her on fire, to boot.

Her phone started its insistent vibrating again.

It was probably her boss at the library, letting her know she was fired. She couldn't blame her if she did. She'd brought serious trouble to the library doors.

Her life was basically all trouble right now...except for Owen.

She checked the screen—unknown number—then cleared her throat and tapped the accept button. "Hello?"

Ignoring any call was out of the question right now.

"Leah."

"Isl—Alyssa." She frowned at the sound of her former roommate's breathing—too rapid, as if she'd been running. "Are you okay? Why are you calling?"

"I'm at the lake house," she whispered. "Someone's here... I need your help. Please."

Leah scrambled out from beneath the covers. The room spun with the sudden movement. "I'll get there as fast as I can. Is there a place you can hide? In the woods? Somewhere?"

She staggered to her closet. Grabbed a pair of jeans from the closet, then a tee. No time for a bra.

"I think so. Hurry, Leah."

The call ended. Leah threw the phone down and quickly dressed. "Owen!" She stuffed her feet into a pair of slides and rushed out of her room.

Owen was headed to her door.

"We have to go. Alyssa is at the lake house and someone's there. She's afraid and hiding."

He nodded. "Let's go."

Leah had started to panic by the time they were in the

car. The idea that it would take them at least fifty minutes to get to the lake house had her nerves tattered.

"The police would get there more quickly," Owen said, reading her mind.

Leah hated the idea of feeling as if she had given up her friend to the police. No, Alyssa—Isla, whatever she called herself—was not really her friend. Leah should know that by now.

"You're right. Should we call Detective Lambert?"

"I'll call him," he said, understanding her hesitancy.

At the next traffic signal, he made the call. When he'd hung up, he glanced at Leah. "Someone will be there in the next ten minutes."

Leah breathed a sigh of relief. No matter what happened, that call was the right thing to do if her former friend's life was truly in danger.

"There's something else."

She turned to him, her heart nearly stalling with worry. "I'm listening."

"The black sedan leased to Douglas's company that has been following you," he said.

"The one with the driver who could be the same person who tried to set me on fire?"

"Considering what they found in the car," Owen said, "I would say so."

"Did they catch him?" She mentally crossed her fingers. Maybe he could provide some answers about who hired him or who else was involved.

"They found the car. He was inside. Dead."

Her hopes sank. "Who was he?"

"They're trying to run that down right now. There was

no ID on him. His wallet was missing. The registration in the glove box shows After Dark."

"How do we know he was the one in the library?"

She wasn't sure she would ever feel completely safe again until he was found.

"His prints. He wasn't in the system until the incident at the library, and since he didn't wear gloves, his prints were on the container of lighter fluid and on the lighter. They matched the ones they took from the dead man. Those same prints were all over the car."

Having anyone be murdered was not something she would ever want...but the idea that she no longer had to worry about that threat was a relief.

But what about who hired him?

Morris Lake House
Fox Lake, 8:15 a.m.

THREE POLICE CRUISERS were in the driveway. Owen parked behind them. One uniform waited at the house, and five others were combing the woods and knocking on neighbors' doors.

Detective Lambert was there too. Leah spotted him getting out of his car.

"I think I'll stay in the car, if that's okay." She didn't want to answer the questions he would have. She didn't want to see her former roommate's body if they'd found it. Leah just needed to stay back for a bit.

Owen glanced toward the back entrance of the house and the officer standing there with Lambert. "I'll leave the car running for the air-conditioning but lock the doors when I get out."

She nodded. "Sure."

Her stomach was tied in knots. This just kept going and going, and she was so, so tired of it all. She released her seat belt and closed her eyes. It was probably the concussion making her feel so weary and irritable. She'd forgotten all about that last night, but this morning had brought the whole nightmare back.

A rap on the glass of the driver's-side door made her eyes snap open. She turned, expecting to see Owen at the door already—not Owen.

Alyssa stared at her through the window, eyes wide. She tugged at the door handle. "Please," she murmured.

Without thinking, Leah hit the unlock button. A glance forward showed Owen and Lambert looking at something on the uniformed officer's cell phone.

Alyssa dropped into the driver's seat, hunkering down as if she feared being seen. "Thank God you came."

Leah sat up straighter. "What's going on?" She looked forward. "I should get Owen. Everyone's looking for you."

"No!" She grabbed Leah's arm. "Please, just listen to me first."

Leah relaxed a tiny fraction. "All right, but I need to know what's really going on. Right now."

Alyssa glanced forward. "If they see me..." Rather than finish the statement, she shoved the gear shift into reverse and barreled out of the driveway.

Leah reached for her door.

"Don't."

She glanced at the woman behind the wheel. There was a gun in her hand, and it was pointed at Leah.

She spun onto the road. "Just relax," she ordered, struggling to control the car with her one free hand.

The beeping sound warned them that the car's fob was with Owen. How far would the vehicle go without it? The warning signal for the fact that neither she nor the driver were wearing seat belts grew louder as well, creating a building staccato.

"What are you doing?" Leah demanded. "Stop the car now. Owen and I are trying to help you."

Her former roommate laughed. "I swear." She whipped the car left, heading down a side road.

Leah slammed against the door, grimaced at the ache in her head, then righted herself.

Alyssa hit the brakes then, and Leah almost slammed into the dash but caught herself. Her aching head screamed in protest. "What the hell are you doing?"

The sound of the door locks disengaging had Leah reaching for her door again. Alyssa nudged her with the gun. "Do not even think about it."

The back door behind Leah opened, and someone got in. Leah turned to see and gaped.

Louise Douglas.

"What is going on?" Leah demanded of the woman behind the wheel.

Alyssa handed the gun to Louise. "Better buckle up."

She slammed on the accelerator. Leah braced herself, hands against the dash, rather than bothering with the seat belt.

"Did you send that man to kill me?" Leah demanded, turning to look over her shoulder at the woman now sitting in the middle of the back seat.

"I did." She grinned. "Too bad he failed. I never could tolerate a man who failed on the follow-through."

The two of them, Louise and Alyssa, laughed.

"Did you kill Raymond too?" Leah asked, fury pounding inside her. She should have been afraid, but instead she was furious. Her head didn't even hurt anymore, or maybe she just couldn't feel it.

"No," the driver said, "that was me." She grinned at Leah. "Don't feel bad for him. He deserved it. He was a womanizing pig."

Leah suddenly realized one thing with complete certainty: they weren't sharing all this information to build comradery...they intended to kill her.

"They'll know it was you." She looked from her former friend to the woman in the back seat.

"Not me," Louise said. She showed off her gloved hands, the gun in one of them. "I was never even here."

Alyssa slowed to look back at her accomplice. "What does that mean?"

Leah took the opportunity to open the door and launch herself out. The jump might gravely injure her, but at least she'd have a shot at surviving. If she stayed in the vehicle, she was certain to end up dead.

She hit the ground hard, rolled to a stop. Then she scrambled to her feet and started to run. Her head was spinning, but she didn't slow down.

Tires squealed as the car started to back up.

Leah had to find a way out of its path before—

Her thought was interrupted by the sound of a gunshot.

OWEN BRAKED TO a stop. "They turned off somewhere?"

Lambert looked over the seat to stare out the rear window. "Back that way, on the left."

Owen slammed into reverse, and the car rocketed backward. When they reached the turn off, he hit the brakes, then shoved into drive, lunging down the narrow road.

The first thing he saw was Leah diving for the ditch.

Then a bullet struck the windshield.

"Get down!" Lambert shouted.

Owen pushed into park and shot out of the car before it stopped rocking. He skirted around to the back of the vehicle for cover. Lambert did the same.

"Cover me." Owen went for the ditch.

Lambert laid down fire to keep the shooter on the other side ducking.

The air didn't fill Owen's lungs again until Leah was within reach. "Keep down and move toward the car. I'll be behind you."

They headed for the car.

A round of shots hit the ground.

Owen was on top of Leah instantly. When Lambert started firing again, he moved, urging Leah forward. They scrambled up the bank and behind the car where Lambert was still spraying bullets toward the other vehicle.

Owen's stolen car suddenly barreled forward.

Lambert stopped firing.

Owen raised his head above the trunk and watched as his car faded into the distance. But it was the woman left in the middle of the road, clambering to her feet, that held his attention. She shouted at the fleeing vehicle.

Lambert stepped away from the vehicle, his weapon aimed at the woman. "Put your hands up!" he shouted.

"Stay down," Owen warned Leah. "Do not move unless you see my car coming from the other direction."

She nodded, her face pale.

Owen stood and followed Lambert.

"She kidnapped me!" Louise Douglas stood in the middle of the road, hands up in surrender. "She was going to kill us both."

Leah was suddenly next to Owen, swaying precariously. "She's lying. She was going to kill me. The two of them are working together."

Before Owen could grab her, Leah stormed up to the other woman. He was right behind her but didn't catch up fast enough to prevent what happened next.

Leah punched the other woman in the face. Louise hit the ground.

"That's for having that guy try to kill me." She rubbed her fist.

"You got this?" Lambert asked, backing toward the car.

"Got it," Owen assured him.

"I'll send a patrol car for the woman, and the rest of us are going to find the one who got away."

Owen helped Douglas to her feet. "If you resist," he warned, "the next punch will be from me."

In the five minutes that followed, a patrol car arrived and took custody of Louise Douglas. Another uniform offered to give them a ride; Owen declined and told the officer to help the others find his car and the fugitive driving it.

When the police were gone, he called the office and ordered a car to pick him and Leah up. Then he draped his arm around her shoulders and pulled her close. She looked ready to drop.

"You okay?"

"I guess so." She leaned her head against him. "I guess I held out hope that Isla—Alyssa, whatever, was telling the truth. That the friendship we shared was real on some level."

But it wasn't. Owen understood how difficult that must be to accept.

"You up to walking for a few minutes?"

"Yeah. I just want to get out of here."

"I can make that happen," he promised. "In fact, I think we're both due for a vacation."

She peered up at him, the new bruise on her cheek making his gut clench. "A vacation sounds amazing."

"Don't you want to know where?" he asked, grinning at her eagerness.

"I don't care where as long as I'm with you."

"Same," he murmured as he leaned down to press a kiss to her forehead.

They walked until their ride arrived, and then they relaxed and started to plan.

Chapter Fifteen

Wednesday, August 27
The Apartment
Chestnut Street, 10:00 a.m.

Leah packed the last of her things into a final box, then glanced around the living room.

Her few pieces of furniture, as well as the ones that had belonged to the real Isla Morris, were being donated to charity. With Isla's mother dead—of an overdose, as Alyssa had suggested—there was no one to take possession of anything. As for the clothes and personal belongings, they had been boxed up for donation as well.

Leah sighed. She was glad to be finished with this part.

She glanced at the time. Owen would be here in a few minutes to pick her up. He'd rented a small moving van for hauling her boxes to the new place. His friend had come through with one of the studio apartments Owen had mentioned. Leah was excited about the move.

She couldn't deny having some regrets about walking away from the last three years of her life, but what else could she do? The friends she'd made had been friends of Alyssa's. They hadn't really cared about Leah. And that was okay. She didn't need those people. She'd recognized their self-centeredness from the beginning, but they were her roommate's friends, so she'd ignored their shortcomings.

Lambert and the Chicago PD had caught Alyssa. She and Louise Douglas were in jail, both charged with murder. The Douglas children were with their grandparents. Leah would never understand how a parent could do this to her children.

Alyssa was spilling her guts in hopes of a deal. Louise had said nothing since her outrageously expensive attorney had counseled her to keep her mouth shut.

Leah had given her statement to Lambert, and she, of course, would have no choice but to testify at the trials as a witness. But until then, she was not looking back.

The woman who had pretended to be Isla Morris's mother had gotten scared and turned herself in. Alyssa had admitted that she and Louise had gotten intimately involved and devised the entire scheme. Now they would both be going to prison. No matter the deal Alyssa wrangled, she was not getting out of a murder charge.

Leah regretted that she had ever believed the woman. But she was a good person, and she'd always believed the best in people. She would have thought she'd learned her lesson with Chris, but apparently not.

She had contacted Bechel at the insurance company and signed over her portion of the insurance proceeds to Raymond's children. Whatever kind of selfish person he had been, he would have wanted his children cared for, Leah felt certain.

The sound of the buzzer announced that Owen had arrived. She rushed to the door and was just about to press the necessary button to grant him entrance when she remembered that there was a possibility it wasn't him. She pressed the intercom button instead. "Yes?"

"It's me," he said.

A smile broke across her lips. She pressed the button that would release the entrance-door lock and then waited just outside her door for him to arrive. When he hit the top of the stairs, her heart started to pound. Watching him walk toward her had the organ racing. She loved the way he walked. Loved every part of him. During their weeklong vacation, he had explored every inch of her and she had done the same to him. Her smile stretched even wider at the beautiful bouquet of flowers he carried.

"You're here," she said, sounding breathless.

"I am." He stopped directly in front of her. "You ready?"

She nodded. "I am so ready." She looked at the flowers. "Are those for me?"

He smiled. "They are. You said no one had ever sent you flowers. I intend to do that as often as possible."

She kissed him, almost crushing the flowers in the process.

They spent the next few minutes carrying boxes to the rented van. When she locked the apartment door for the last time, she turned to Owen.

"I'm glad this is behind me."

He smiled. "Me too."

"But the best part—" she reached for him, slid her arms around his waist "—is what's in front of me."

He leaned down and kissed her.

She could not wait to see where their journey took them next.

The Colby Agency, 7:30 p.m.

VICTORIA SHUT OFF the light to her office and closed the door. It had been a long day, but a very good one. Several investigations were settled, and all investigators and clients were safe. This was always what she hoped for. When love bloomed between an investigator and a client, it was all the better.

The Colby Agency had a long history of solving the most difficult cases as well as bringing some amazing people together.

Victoria was very proud of her agency and of all who'd worked here, past and present. They were all such great people. In all the years she had been at the head of this agency, she had only ever lost one investigator and that was one too many. The many, many clients they had helped often sent postcards or letters of thanks even years later.

Victoria truly loved the agency and the work they did.

She smiled as she reached the lobby. Lucas waited there for her. She should have known Jamie would call him. She hadn't wanted to leave this evening without Victoria. Everyone else had gone. But Victoria had needed some time alone at her beloved window, watching life on the street below. Not that she had any troubles to worry about. No. Life was well within the Colby family. But there were times when she just needed to stare out that window and remember all the times she had done so before.

This evening had been one of those times.

The sight of Lucas waiting for her lifted her nostalgic heart. No matter that they were both getting up there agewise, she still saw him as the dashing man who had stolen her heart when she had been certain her heart would never again feel that kind of love.

Like James, her first husband, Lucas had been a master spy, his work the darkest of dark operations. He, James and Victoria had been dear friends for a lifetime before tragedy stuck so very hard. First, her son had been abducted, and then her husband had been murdered. Before James's death, they had desperately searched for their child. She regretted so that James had not lived to see their son returned. Jim was a good, strong man.

He hadn't returned to Victoria that way, however. Jim had been horribly abused and brainwashed. He had come back to her as a killer, determined to murder her. But somehow she had reached him and he had changed. Over the years since that time, he had married and had two beautiful children. One of which, Jamie, now worked with Victoria, running the agency. Luke, the younger of the two, was in medical school.

Life was as perfect as could be expected in this changing world.

"I thought," Lucas announced, "that I would take you to dinner, my love."

Victoria put her arm in his and turned to the elevator. "I think that is an amazing idea." She grinned. "Jamie called you, didn't she?"

He grinned as well. "She did. She said you were looking a little sad."

Victoria rose onto her tiptoes and gave him a kiss on the jaw. "Not sad, just lost in memories."

The elevator doors opened and they stepped into the car.

"I hope I was present in those memories."

"You, my dear husband, are in the very best of all my memories, going back to the night we met."

"The night James stole you away from me," he teased.

Victoria laughed. Lucas swore to this day that he had been smitten with Victoria, but it was James who had swept her off her feet that long-ago night when they were all so young.

"But you were always there," she reminded him. "Always a part of our lives, for better or worse."

He nodded. "I was, indeed."

"Thank you, Lucas." When he met her gaze with a questioning look, she explained, "For being the man who helped me love again."

"No thanks necessary, my dear. I was happy to wait for that moment."

The doors closed and the elevator swept them down to the lobby.

When the doors opened once more, rather than finding an empty space where only the security guard manned the information desk, she found a room full of people. She gasped. Not just people. Everyone from the agency... even some she hadn't seen in years. And the massive lobby was decorated beautifully with balloons and flowers and streamers.

"What on earth?" she murmured.

"Happy birthday, Victoria," Lucas said, turning to her. "I hope this one is the best one yet."

Jim and Tasha, Jamie and Luke, they hurried forward and hugged her. Despite her best efforts, tears filled Victoria's eyes.

"You didn't say a word," she said to Jamie.

Jamie grinned. "It was a surprise, Grandmother." She

gestured to a small stage that had been erected with a waiting microphone.

Victoria surveyed the clapping crowd as they urged her to speak.

"Come along," Lucas said, ushering her toward the stage. "They're all waiting to hear from you."

Victoria stepped up onto the stage and scanned the crowd. She smiled. Lucas didn't have to worry. This was certainly the best birthday ever.

* * * * *

Look for Striking Distance *and read the suspense-filled story of Jim Colby's return.*

Get up to 4 Free Books!

**We'll send you 2 free books from each series you try
PLUS a free Mystery Gift.**

FREE Value Over **$25**

Both the **Harlequin Intrigue®** and **Harlequin® Romantic Suspense** series feature compelling novels filled with heart-racing action-packed romance that will keep you on the edge of your seat.

YES! Please send me 2 FREE novels from the Harlequin Intrigue or Harlequin Romantic Suspense series and my FREE gift (gift is worth about $10 retail). After receiving them, if I don't wish to receive any more books, I can return the shipping statement marked "cancel." If I don't cancel, I will receive 6 brand-new Harlequin Intrigue Larger-Print books every month and be billed just $7.19 each in the U.S. or $7.99 each in Canada, or 4 brand-new Harlequin Romantic Suspense books every month and be billed just $6.39 each in the U.S. or $7.19 each in Canada, a savings of 20% off the cover price. It's quite a bargain! Shipping and handling is just 50¢ per book in the U.S. and $1.25 per book in Canada.* I understand that accepting the 2 free books and gift places me under no obligation to buy anything. I can always return a shipment and cancel at any time by calling the number below. The free books and gift are mine to keep no matter what I decide.

Choose one:
- ☐ **Harlequin Intrigue Larger-Print** (199/399 BPA G36Y)
- ☐ **Harlequin Romantic Suspense** (240/340 BPA G36Y)
- ☐ **Or Try Both!** (199/399 & 240/340 BPA G36Z)

Name (please print)

Address   Apt. #

City   State/Province   Zip/Postal Code

Email: Please check this box ☐ if you would like to receive newsletters and promotional emails from Harlequin Enterprises ULC and its affiliates. You can unsubscribe anytime.

Mail to the Harlequin Reader Service:
IN U.S.A.: P.O. Box 1341, Buffalo, NY 14240-8531
IN CANADA: P.O. Box 603, Fort Erie, Ontario L2A 5X3

Want to explore our other series or interested in ebooks? **Visit www.ReaderService.com or call 1-800-873-8635.**

*Terms and prices subject to change without notice. Prices do not include sales taxes, which will be charged (if applicable) based on your state or country of residence. Canadian residents will be charged applicable taxes. Offer not valid in Quebec. This offer is limited to one order per household. Books received may not be as shown. Not valid for current subscribers to the Harlequin Intrigue or Harlequin Romantic Suspense series. All orders subject to approval. Credit or debit balances in a customer's account(s) may be offset by any other outstanding balance owed by or to the customer. Please allow 4 to 6 weeks for delivery. Offer available while quantities last.

Your Privacy—Your information is being collected by Harlequin Enterprises ULC, operating as Harlequin Reader Service. For a complete summary of the information we collect, how we use this information and to whom it is disclosed, please visit our privacy notice located at https://corporate.harlequin.com/privacy-notice. Notice to California Residents – Under California law, you have specific rights to control and access your data. For more information on these rights and how to exercise them, visit https://corporate.harlequin.com/california-privacy. For additional information for residents of other U.S. states that provide their residents with certain rights with respect to personal data, visit https://corporate.harlequin.com/other-state-residents-privacy-rights/.

HIHRS25